**Her Mediterranean Playboy
Sexy and dangerous—
he wants you in his bed!**

The sky is blue, the azure sea is crashing against
the golden sand and the sun is hot.

The conditions are perfect for a scorching
Mediterranean seduction from two irresistible
untamed playboys!

Indulge your senses with these two delicious
stories from Melanie Milburne and Kate Hewitt.

D0836982

All about the authors...

MELANIE MILBURNE: I am married to a surgeon and live in Hobart, Tasmania, where I enjoy an active life as a long-distance runner and a nationally ranked top-ten swimmer in Australia. I also have a master's degree in education. When not running or swimming I write, and when I'm not doing all of the above I'm reading.

KATE HEWITT wrote her first story at the age of five. That story was one sentence long—fortunately they've become a bit more detailed as she's grown older.

She has written plays, short stories and magazine serials for many years, but writing romance remains her first love. Besides writing, she enjoys reading, traveling and learning to knit.

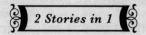

2 Stories in 1

Melanie Milburne
Kate Hewitt

HER MEDITERRANEAN
PLAYBOY

HARLEQUIN®

TORONTO • NEW YORK • LONDON
AMSTERDAM • PARIS • SYDNEY • HAMBURG
STOCKHOLM • ATHENS • TOKYO • MILAN • MADRID
PRAGUE • WARSAW • BUDAPEST • AUCKLAND

If you purchased this book without a cover you should be aware that this book is stolen property. It was reported as "unsold and destroyed" to the publisher, and neither the author nor the publisher has received any payment for this "stripped book."

Recycling programs
for this product may
not exist in your area.

ISBN-13: 978-0-373-12910-2

HER MEDITERRANEAN PLAYBOY
Copyright © 2010 by Harlequin Enterprises Ltd.

First North American Publication 2010.

The publisher acknowledges the copyright holders of the individual works as follows:

MISTRESS AT THE ITALIAN'S COMMAND
Copyright © 2008 by Melanie Milburne.

ITALIAN BOSS, HOUSEKEEPER MISTRESS
Copyright © 2009 by Kate Hewitt.

All rights reserved. Except for use in any review, the reproduction or utilization of this work in whole or in part in any form by any electronic, mechanical or other means, now known or hereafter invented, including xerography, photocopying and recording, or in any information storage or retrieval system, is forbidden without the written permission of the publisher, Harlequin Enterprises Limited, 225 Duncan Mill Road, Don Mills, Ontario, Canada M3B 3K9.

This is a work of fiction. Names, characters, places and incidents are either the product of the author's imagination or are used fictitiously, and any resemblance to actual persons, living or dead, business establishments, events or locales is entirely coincidental.

This edition published by arrangement with Harlequin Books S.A.

® and TM are trademarks of the publisher. Trademarks indicated with ® are registered in the United States Patent and Trademark Office, the Canadian Trade Marks Office and in other countries.

www.eHarlequin.com

Printed in U.S.A.

CONTENTS

Mistress at the Italian's Command
Melanie Milburne

CHAPTER ONE

'MISS ALICE BENTON?' The Italian psychiatrist took Ally to one side, speaking in a grave, heavily accented tone. 'Do you have any idea how long your sister has been off her medication?'

Ally swallowed against the dry lump of anguish in her throat. 'I'm really not sure,' she said. 'I don't live in Italy with my sister. I live in Australia.'

'Then you did well to get here so soon.' He looked down at the notes and added, 'She was only brought in yesterday morning by her neighbour.'

'I had a business meeting in Prague,' Ally explained. 'I flew from there as soon as I could. I had no idea she'd had such a bad relapse. She hasn't had one in years. She was fine when I spoke to her from Sydney before I left for my trip. I can't believe—' she choked over a sob '—she would do something like this. She seemed so…so well…'

'This was a very serious suicide attempt,' Dr Bassano said with a sober look. 'She was lucky to survive such a high dosage of benzoates. I suggest that until she is stabilised on her regular dosage of anti-psychotic medication that she be admitted to a mental health clinic and stay there until she receives the therapy and rehabilitation she needs. I should warn you, however, it could take considerable time.'

'I see…' Ally said, feeling her stomach sink even lower in despair. She had desperately hoped the frightening see-sawing periods of mania and dark depression her sister had suffered ever since she was fifteen had finally disappeared, but it seemed they had not. What on earth had happened in her sister's life to bring on such a devastating relapse?

'There is a clinic in Switzerland that has a very good reputation.' Dr Bassano interrupted the painful torture of Ally's thoughts. 'It is a private clinic, but well worth the expense. The staff are all highly trained and very empathetic.'

Ally moistened her parched lips with the tip of her tongue. 'But can't I take her back to Sydney with me?' she asked. 'Surely it would be better for her to be back home? She's been abroad for almost a year. Perhaps that's what's caused this…this…crisis.'

'Miss Benton, I do not think your sister is in any fit state to endure a long-haul flight,' he said. 'In my opinion it would do more harm than good. She is unstable, and I suspect has been so for quite some time. The Swiss clinic is only a short flight or train journey away. We can arrange for a health professional to accompany both of you to settle her in.'

Ally compressed her lips to keep her panic contained. 'H-how long do you think she will need to be at this clinic you have recommended?' she asked.

'It takes time for the medication to kick in again, sometimes several weeks,' he paused, then went on gravely. 'In more difficult cases maybe even months, especially if a drug change is indicated, which I suspect in your sister's case is indeed warranted. There are several new medications on the market now that specifically target her condition. It would be worth a few weeks of trialling one or two of them in a safe environment to see which is most efficacious.'

Ally looked at the specialist in alarm. She only had a couple of weeks' leave. She had been so looking forward to the holiday she had planned with her sister. She had never for a moment imagined it would turn into such a nightmare as this. There had been no warning, no sign of anything untoward during any of their recent phone conversations or e-mails. Admittedly her sister had sounded overly excited recently, but Ally had put it down to the anticipation of spending two weeks relaxing in the sun together. She hadn't dared think of any other explanation. Alex's troubled past had been filed away in Ally's head; the door was not locked but it was certainly not ajar, as it had been for so long during their adolescence and early adult years.

Alex had done some terribly impulsive things during her various manic stages, and Ally was still trying to clear the debt of some of the mad spending sprees her twin had gone on in the past. Her sister's disastrous marriage to Darren Sharpe had been the lowest point. It had taken Ally months to convince her twin to leave her abusive husband, and even longer to rebuild her battered self-esteem once the divorce was finalised.

'I think Alex will do quite well once this crisis is over, but it is important that over the next few weeks she is kept away from any stressful situations,' Dr Bassano said. 'Stress at this point in time will only intensify her condition and perhaps cause another relapse. I have been in contact with her specialist in Sydney. I see from her records she has already had three major breakdowns during her teens. I would like to avoid triggering another one.'

'I understand,' Ally said, fighting back tears.

Dr Bassano took Ally's hand. 'I realise how difficult this is for you, Miss Benton,' he said. 'I understand you have been responsible for your sister since your mother's death. You have done an amazing job of supporting her thus far. You must not blame yourself for this latest relapse. It is always hard for close relatives. You cannot possibly be with her every minute of the day. You have your own life to lead and must be allowed to do so.'

Ally blinked back the moisture in her eyes. 'Thank y-you,' she said, her voice catching slightly. 'I don't want to lose her...she is all I have...'

'Take care of yourself,' Dr Bassano said gently. 'Your sister is still sleeping, but should wake in the next hour or so. Please call me at any time if you have any further questions.'

Ally went back to her sister's bedside and looked down at the pale, thin and wan mirror image of herself, curled up like a helpless infant on the narrow bed.

How could two identical people be so dissimilar? she wondered. Alex had always been the outgoing one, the extroverted talkative one, the girl men flocked to like bees around nectar-laden blossom.

Ally, on the other hand, had always preferred her own company to that of other people. With the same figure and features of her twin, she had her fair share of male attention, but no one had come close enough for her to let down the guard around her heart. The emotional blunting in her childhood had seen to that. Living with an unpredictable mother had made Ally naturally cautious. She found it hard to trust people and kept herself aloof and on guard— unlike her twin who, like their mother, often leapt in feet first with little regard for the consequences.

The sheets on the bed rustled and a croaky voice asked, 'Ally…is that you?'

Ally leaned forward and took her sister's hands in hers, squeezing them gently. 'Yes, darling, it's me. I came as soon as I could.'

'I'm sorry…' Alex's face began to crumple. 'I've really done it this time. You're going to hate me…I just know it…I've ruined everything…'

'No, darling, don't talk like that,' Ally soothed, still desperately trying not to cry. 'I could never hate you. You know I would do anything to make you well again.'

'He told me he loved me…' Alex said, so softly Ally had trouble hearing her.

She leaned even closer. 'Who told you he loved you?'

Alex's eyes closed and a soft whimper escaped from her lips. 'I don't want to talk about it…it hurts so much…'

Ally stroked her sister's hand. 'Don't upset yourself, honey. We can talk later. The important thing now is to get well. That's all that matters.'

'The doctor said I have to go to a clinic,' Alex said, biting her lip like a small, insecure child.

'Yes, it will be for the best,' Ally said. 'Don't worry about the expense. I'll see to it.'

Tears sprouted from Alex's eyes. 'I wanted to die… I felt that if I couldn't have him what would be the point in going on?'

Ally felt yet again the tight fist of panic knocking hard on the door of her heart. The doctor had warned her not to allow her twin to suffer any unnecessary stress, but clearly something had been going on with a man while Alex had been living abroad.

'Honey, you should have told me you were having trouble coping,' Ally said gently. 'I thought everything was going so well for you since you moved to London.'

Alex's sapphire-blue gaze shifted to stare blankly at the hem of the sheet covering her chest. 'I didn't want to tell you because I knew you'd disapprove.'

'Why would I do that, darling?' Ally asked, although deep down she felt sure she already knew the answer.

'He's married,' Alex said, confirming Ally's suspicions. 'I didn't realise that until I'd thrown in my job and followed him to Rome. He told me he loved me. He even told me he was going to leave his wife. But it was all a lie…'

Ally inwardly sighed. She needed more than her fingers and toes to count the number of affairs with married men her sister had been involved in over the years. Alex seemed to misread the signals, or something. She was so easily taken in by a charming smile and ended up disappointed and betrayed time and time again. But this one seemed to have had a much more devastating effect, and Ally wished she could press for more details. But she knew it would probably do more harm than good at this point.

'When did you stop taking your tablets?' she asked, diverting the subject.

Alex closed her eyes. 'I don't remember…a few weeks ago, I think. I didn't want him to know I was taking medication. I thought he wouldn't love me if he thought I wasn't…you know…normal.'

'Alex you *are* normal,' Ally insisted. 'If you had asthma or diabetes you'd have to take regular medication. How is your mental condition any different?'

Alex's eyes remained closed. 'But I feel crazy. My head is full of racing thoughts. I feel out of control, and that's why…' She gave another defeated sigh. 'What's the point? What's done is done.'

'Darling, remember the doctors back home told you how important it is for you take your tablets regularly?' Ally said, trying to remain patient and calm. 'This time in the clinic will be just the thing for you. You'll be able to get on top of things, both medically and personally.'

Alex turned her head back to look at Ally. 'Do you really still love me, Ally? Even after all I've put you through? I'm a terrible person. I hate myself. I can't do anything right. I ruin everything.'

'That's rubbish, Alex, and you know it,' Ally said. 'You'll come through this. I know you will. You know I love you, and nothing can change that. You and me together against the world, right?'

Alex bit her lower lip and shifted her gaze again. 'I don't really want to end up like Mum…but I just can't seem to help it. It must be genetic—but then you have the same genes and you're fine…'

Ally pushed aside the giant wave of survival guilt that instantly swamped her, and grasped her sister's hand again. 'Mum didn't get the help she needed,' she said. 'She was sick for a long time, but we were too young to realise it. Her up-and-down moods and her erratic behaviour seemed a part of who she was. There's a fine line between personality and mental illness, Alex. It's hard even for the professionals to know when patients cross it.'

Alex turned her head on the pillow to look at her. 'I've done some terrible things,' she said, her eyes swelling with tears. 'I just couldn't seem to stop myself. I wanted to get back at Rocco for…for everything…'

'Rocco was the man you were having an affair with?' Ally asked, trying to string the pieces together without pushing too hard.

Alex's eyes welled again with tears and her bottom lip began to tremble uncontrollably. 'I can't talk about it…I just can't…'

Ally stroked her sister's hand. 'That's fine, honey. I understand. We'll leave it for another time, when you're feeling better.'

Alex let out a defeated sigh and closed her eyes wearily. 'I'll go to the clinic,' she said. 'I want to get well. I can't go on like this. I know I've been a dreadful burden for you in the past. I wanted to make you proud of me, living independently and working abroad. I thought I could do it. But…but I guess this is my last chance to put things right.'

'Darling it's *not* your last chance. There is no such thing as last chances,' Ally said, pressing a tender kiss to her twin's forehead. 'Besides, what if the shoe was on the other foot?'

Alex opened one bleary eye to look at her. 'What do you mean?'

'We're identical twins,' Ally said. 'Like you said before, we share exactly the same DNA but by chance you have developed an illness that needs carefully managed treatment. It could just as easily be me in that bed, not you.'

Alex opened both of her dark blue eyes and looked at her sister with gravitas. 'You should be thanking God you don't have to step into my shoes,' she said. 'I wouldn't wish my life on anyone, not after what I've done. I feel so…so guilty.'

'I don't have to step into your shoes to understand what you are going through,' Ally said. 'But let me tell you if I had to I would do it, and do it gladly.'

Alex attempted a smile, but it was a bit crooked and tinged with aching sadness. 'Just as well we're the same size, then, huh?'

CHAPTER TWO

ALLY had not long returned to Rome from her trip, having settled her twin sister into the quiet sanctuary of the clinic in Switzerland, when the doorbell of her sister's rented apartment sounded. She had come back there to do a rudimentary clean-up, knowing Alex would be out of town for possibly weeks if not months on end, and had decided a refrigerator clean-out was probably a good idea, not to mention a load or two of washing and a bed linen change before she arranged to travel back to Zurich.

What she hadn't expected to find was a rather nasty eviction notice and a demand for six weeks' rent in arrears, with a letter written in Italian that looked as if it was from a lawyer. But what Ally couldn't understand was why her sister had neglected to pay the rent, for as she was folding Alex's clothes in the bedroom she had come across a large amount of money, tied in neat bundles and placed inside a jacket pocket. Uncertain of what to do with such a sum, Ally had placed it in her handbag until she could consult her sister.

The doorbell rang again, this time with a little more force, so Ally pushed the papers and the rest of her sister's unpaid bills to one side and, giving the newly made-up bed a quick straighten, made her way to the front door. She opened it to find a tall, dark-haired man standing there, his stance autocratic and his gaze very determined as it locked down on hers.

'Mrs Alexandra Sharpe?'

Ally stared back at the bottomless brown eyes boring down

into hers and felt a shiver of apprehension shimmy up her spine. 'Look…if it's about the rent I can explain—'

He slanted one dark eyebrow at her. 'Don't tell me you have forgotten me already?' he said. 'I know we only met the once, but surely I am not that forgettable?'

'Um… I… Um…' Ally was at a loss for words.

'Perhaps I should refresh your memory?' he said with a contemptuous set to his mouth. 'You gatecrashed a business function my brother-in-law Rocco Montano and I attended three weeks ago. Your behaviour created quite a stir. Had I known then what I know now I would have personally evicted you from the premises, instead of engaging Security to do it for me.'

Ally stared at him with wide eyes. She wasn't sure if she should tell him who she was or go along with his assumption that she was Alex. She suddenly felt as if she was on a set of delicately balanced scales. A tilt one way could clear away the confusion; the other could cause catastrophic results…

Or would it?

Once the thought had blossomed in her brain she couldn't quite get rid of it. Had Alex ever mentioned to her lover about having an identical twin? she wondered.

She stared at the man's classically handsome features as her heart did a hopscotch routine in her chest. 'You seem sort of vaguely familiar,' she said, to fill the silence.

'May I come in?' he asked, although Ally felt it was more of a command than a request.

She opened the door and he moved past her before she could balance the scales of reason in her scrambled brain.

He was very tall, towering over her five foot eight height, and he had long legs and broad shoulders which were a perfect hanger for the Italian designed suit he was wearing. His neither long nor short casually styled black hair was as glossy as a raven's wing, brushed backwards—although not willingly, it seemed, as a thick strand seemed to fall forward across his forehead almost every time he moved. One of his hands moved upwards to shove it back, the action so automatic Ally couldn't help feeling it was almost unconscious. He probably did it a hundred times a day and didn't realise.

His eyes were a brownish black, fringed with thick sooty lashes that acted like a screen over his fathomless gaze as it collided with hers. He was the most strikingly handsome man she had ever met. He exuded power and male potency from every olive-toned pore of his body. His mouth was full and sensual, his blade of a nose distinctly Roman. However, his strongly chiselled jaw had a hint of stubborn arrogance about it, as if he liked his own way and did everything he could to achieve it.

'My name, in case you have forgotten, is Vittorio Vassallo,' he said. 'But I think I do not need to tell you why I am here, *sì*?'

Ally felt her skin involuntarily tighten at the sound of that deep velvet-toned voice, its clear-cut diction indicating English was not his preferred tongue even though he spoke it fluently, as if he had been educated abroad. Oxford or Cambridge, she guessed. His name rang a tiny bell at the back of her brain. On the flight over from Sydney she had read an article about a high-flying Italian billionaire fund manager who had a reputation as an international playboy. Looking at him now, Ally could see why women all over the world fell over themselves to be his mistress.

'Um…now is not really a good time…' she faltered.

He hooked one dark brow upwards in a derisory arc. 'You have another commitment right now?'

She rolled her lips together before moistening them with the tip of her tongue. 'Um…no, but I don't see what possible reason you could have for being here.'

'Do you not?' The dark brow was still slanted upwards, the black-brown gaze unwavering as it held hers.

Ally knew she should probably tell him who she was. Now was the time, before things went any further, but for some reason she felt compelled to find out why he was here before she revealed her identity. She wanted to know what he had planned to say to her sister. What would it hurt to step into her sister's shoes for the next few minutes? Besides, his imperious stance annoyed her. He was looking down at her as if she was a guttersnipe, and that really irked her. Her sister was suffering a mental illness. She did not deserve to be ridiculed or threatened, or at least not while Ally could prevent it. Besides, she wanted to know if he knew what had gone on between his brother-in-law and Alex, and it seemed this was as good a way as any.

'I have no idea why you are here,' she said, in a deliberately haughty tone.

A mocking smile tilted his mouth. 'Rocco warned me you liked to play the dumb blonde role,' he said. 'But that is how you get men to do what you want, is it not? You woo them with those dark blue bedroom eyes and that delectable body of yours. No wonder you have the reputation you have. Few men would be able to resist what you have on offer.'

Ally felt a tinge of pink seep into her cheeks. It was almost laughable, the picture he had painted of her, but she let the charade continue a little longer. She figured it would be worth it to eventually throw his misplaced assumptions back in his supercilious face. She was even starting to enjoy herself. What a shock he would get when he found out he had singled out the wrong target for his disgusting vilification.

She tilted her hip in a provocative fashion and batted her eyelashes at him. 'So what do you think I have on offer, Mr Vassallo?' she asked.

She watched as his dark and disconcertingly penetrating gaze roved her form from head to foot, slowly, deliberately lingering over the baby blue top that snugly outlined the curves of her breasts, going down over her trim waist and slim jean-clad thighs before returning to her face, all without saying a single word.

Ally had never felt more acutely aware of her body. She felt as if he had reached out and touched her all over with his long tanned fingers. Every curve, every pleasure point and every secret place felt invaded by his commanding physical presence. Every fine hair on her body lifted, and her skin crawled with a prickly sensation. Her stomach began to dip and dive erratically as her senses were set alight by the slow burn of his dark gaze as it drifted over her in that annoyingly indolent fashion. Her breasts started to swell and tingle beneath the light cotton of her top, and her breathing was choppy, her chest rising and falling like a damaged set of bellows, making her feel light-headed and terrifyingly out of her depth.

She suddenly realised there was a photograph on the wall unit behind him. If he turned around he would see how he was being played for a fool. It was one she had given her sister after their twenty-fourth birthday last year, just before Alex had flown to London. Ally had set the camera on remote control and captured them smiling, with their arms wrapped around each other. She remembered Alex had commented at the time how they must have done exactly that in their mother's womb, curled up like little angels waiting to be summoned to earth. It had been such a happy night of celebrating, just the two of them. Ally had thought back then—was it only a few months ago?—that her sister was finally on the road to recovery.

Her upper lip broke out in tiny beads of perspiration; she could feel nervous moisture trickling down between her shoulderblades as the silence stretched and stretched like a crevasse being prised apart with giant mechanical jaws.

'Um…would you like a drink?' She said the first thing that popped into her mind.

His brows moved together and he cocked his head at a suspicious angle. 'A drink?'

'Yes,' she said over-brightly, carefully back-stepping towards the kitchen, hoping he would take the hint and follow her. 'I was just about to get one myself. It's very hot for September, don't you think?'

'It is usually still quite hot at this time of year,' he answered, still watching her closely. 'It will not cool down for another week or two at the very least.'

Ally went to the meagre pantry and took out a container of long-life orange juice, trying to control the slight tremble of her hands as she did so. 'I'm sorry I don't have any ice,' she said, turning to face him again. 'I've just been cleaning out the fridge.'

His dark eyes were like twin drills as they bored into hers. 'Are you going away somewhere?'

She pasted a tight smile on her face. 'I'm just doing a bit of a spring clean—out with the old and in with the new, that sort of thing.'

Ally watched as his eyes swept over the small galley kitchen with its tired appliances. 'Have you lived in this apartment long?' he asked, bringing his gaze back to hers.

'Er…a few weeks,' she said, shifting her gaze to pour two glasses of juice. Some of it, in spite of her efforts to control the tremble of her hands, splashed onto the bench. 'I'd like to move to something a little more convenient, but rents are high in the nicer areas.' She handed him a glass of juice. 'Would you excuse me for a moment? I think I can hear one of the taps dripping in the bathroom. It does that now and again.'

'Would you like me to fix it for you?'

Ally stared at him in thinly disguised horror. Of all the things he could have said, that was the last she had expected. He was a billionaire. He probably wouldn't recognise a spanner or a wrench if he was hit over the head with one. But then he wasn't a plumber any more than she had a leaky tap, she reminded herself wryly. 'Er…no, there's really nothing wrong with it,' she said, trying not to sound as flustered as she felt. 'It's just that I didn't turn if off hard enough when I heard the doorbell. I won't be a minute.'

Vittorio took a sip of the room-temperature reconstituted orange juice and grimaced. He thought longingly of his own orange groves on the hills behind his Positano holiday villa, where his housekeeper squeezed fresh fruit daily when he was in residence.

He put the glass down on the chipped counter and cast his gaze around once more. It was no wonder Alex Sharpe was looking for a meal ticket. Her flat was tiny and in desperate need of a makeover. The curtains at the kitchen window were faded and grease-splattered, and the linoleum on the floor was buckled and cracked in places. From what he had seen of the small sitting room the carpet was an out-of-date swirly pattern that would have been at home in the seventies. The furniture too was of a similar design and vintage.

But it was no wonder his weak and womanising brother-in-law had fallen under her spell, he thought. She was lethally attractive. Even dressed as she was in faded jeans, and with her silver-blonde hair in a haphazard knot on top of her head and no make-up on, she was temptation personified. She oozed sensuality. It was in every curve of her body: the long elegant limbs, the delightfully ripe globes of her breasts, the tiny waist and the sexy flare of her hips. Her mouth was blood-red, not from lipstick but from the inbuilt passion she exuded from every fragrant pore of her body. He had smelt the seductive musk and heady fragrance of jasmine clinging to her golden skin as soon as she had opened the door. It had not only filled his nostrils, it had filled his head, and upended his thoughts until he'd had trouble recalling his mission.

He smiled to himself as he thought of his plan to divert the press's attention from Rocco in order to protect his sister Chiara. It was going to be much easier than he had expected. Mrs Alex Sharpe was just the sort of woman who would jump at the chance to improve her circumstances.

Besides, he wasn't going to give her a choice.

Ally rushed through the rest of the flat and grabbed the few photos her sister had displayed and hid them in her suitcase under the bed. She took a couple of steadying breaths and made her way back out to the kitchen. Vittorio Vassallo turned when she came in, his dark gaze meshing with hers.

'Mrs Sharpe—' he began.

'Ally,' she said, mentally cringing at the thought of being addressed by the name of her sister's violent ex-husband. 'I prefer to be called Ally, if you don't mind.'

'My brother-in-law always referred to you as Alexandra or Alex,' he said, his eyes narrowing slightly.

Ally wrestled with herself to hold his penetrating gaze. 'You said your name is Vittorio,' she countered. 'That seems rather a mouthful. What do your friends and family call you?'

'Vito,' he answered. 'But only very close friends and immediate family members call me that.'

'So, Mr Vassallo,' she said giving him a cool little smile, 'how can I be of assistance to you?'

His expression was imperious, condescending almost, which infuriated Ally even further. 'I am here about my car,' he said.

Ally looked at him blankly, her heart starting to kick against her sternum in alarm. 'Your c-car?'

His eyes burned into hers. 'Yes,' he said. 'The car you scraped all over with a key or a nail file, causing several thousand euros worth of damage. It was not my brother-in-law's, as you thought, but mine. I expect you to pay for it.'

Ally swallowed convulsively. 'Um…look…I think you've got the wrong person. I'm not who you think I—'

He stepped closer, almost touching her in the small space of the tawdry kitchen. 'Do you realise I can have you sent to prison for this alone, not to mention the issue of the money you stole?' he asked in a biting tone.

Ally blinked at him. *The money?* What money? What did he mean…? She felt her insides turn to liquid as she suddenly remembered.

The money currently in *her* handbag.

Her knees began to knock together slightly. She dragged in a breath that felt as if it had a bramble attached as the scorch of his accusing gaze held her fast. 'I didn't do it,' she said, her head spinning at his closeness. 'I—I didn't deface your car, and I…I don't know anything about any money.'

He let out a vicious swear word in his mother tongue. Even though Ally only knew a few phrases of Italian she knew it was an expletive just by the sheer force of its delivery. 'You think I do not have proof?' he barked at her savagely.

Ally wanted to tell him who she really was, but knew if she did so he might press charges on Alex, in spite of her fragile mental state. He certainly looked angry and ruthless enough to do so, and until she knew what Alex was being accused of she had no choice but to continue with her artifice.

'W-what sort of proof?' she asked, backing away as far as the kitchen counter would allow, her spine feeling as if it was being sawn in half by the pressure of the counter digging into it from behind.

'We will deal with the car issue first,' he said in a flint-like tone. 'You were photographed by a passer-by on a camera phone.' He reached inside his jacket pocket, took out a slim envelope and handed it to her.

Ally took it with fingers that felt as if the bones and ligaments had been taken out, making the task of opening the envelope almost impossible without betraying her trepidation. But somehow she finally managed to take out the three shots of her twin, which clearly showed her gouging the shiny red paintwork of a top-model Ferrari with what seemed to be a key. Ally had no idea what had made her sister act in such a destructive way, but if the look on her face was any indication Alex had been totally out of control, with a rage so intense her eyes looked wild and her whole demeanour dangerous.

If only Ally knew what had been going on! What had caused her sister to fall apart emotionally? Alex had had numerous break-ups with boyfriends in the past, and while each one had upset her it had never been on this sort of scale. Why had this one caused such a reaction?

'Are you still going to stand there and deny it was you?' he asked.

Ally let out a scratchy sigh and put the photos back inside the envelope. She handed them to him. 'There doesn't seem much point, does there?' she said, mentally resigning herself to the task of maintaining the charade a little longer.

He put the envelope back inside his jacket pocket, still holding her gaze. 'Now,' he said, 'we come to the issue of the money.'

Ally disguised a lumpy swallow. 'I don't know what you're talking about.'

His eyes were like black diamonds as they tethered hers. 'Three days ago Rocco was in possession of a large sum of company funds which he was intending to take to the bank. He told me you intercepted him, and that rather than cause a scene on the street he agreed to talk to you in the privacy of a nearby hotel room. After spending a short period of time with him you disappeared—along with the money.'

Ally felt her stomach drop in alarm. 'I'm not sure why that necessarily means I am responsible,' she said, pushing her chin up defiantly. 'Anyone could have taken it. Rocco included.'

His top lip lifted in an arc of derision. 'Rocco might not be my favourite brother-in-law, but he is a valuable asset to my investment company. I employed him because of his financial acuity. I have never had a moment's doubt about his profession-alism. If he says you stole the money I have no reason not to believe him.'

Ally had to think on her feet, and fast. The money was burning a hole in her handbag and he had only to insist on searching the flat to find it. Her sister would not escape the heavy hand of the law—especially as she was to all intents and purposes a visitor to the country. A theft on that scale would not be overlooked. Certainly not if Vittorio Vassallo had his arrogant way about it.

'It's his word against mine,' she said, throwing him a challeng-ing glare. 'If you go public about this I'll give my own interview to the press on how your brother-in-law seduced me. I'm sure that will go down a treat with all your high-flying investors.'

Anger exploded in his dark gaze. 'You conniving little bitch,' he ground out. 'That's exactly the sort of thing you *would* do—which is why I am here to do everything in my power to stop you.'

Ally straightened her spine, even though her legs beneath it wobbled alarmingly. 'You don't scare me, Mr Vassallo.'

His eyes glittered dangerously. 'Give me time, Mrs Sharpe,' he drawled. 'Just give me time.'

The ensuing silence was so tense the air crackled with it.

Ally stood as still as her trembling body would allow. There was a roaring in her ears, a sinking feeling in her stomach, and a tight band of tension around her forehead at the thought of taking Vittorio Vassallo on in a battle she couldn't possibly hope to win.

She was outclassed.

She was out of her depth.

She was a fraud…

'Rocco informed me you left your job in London to follow him here. Is that correct?' he asked.

Ally tried not to fidget under his piercing scrutiny. 'Er…yes.'

'So you are currently unemployed. Is that also correct?' he asked.

'That is correct,' she lied, her conscience not even niggling her this time. Why should it? she thought. She was on leave for the next two weeks, so technically she wasn't working.

'I have a proposition for you,' he said into the ringing silence.

Ally lifted her chin to a pugnacious height. 'Oh, really?'

'My brother-in-law has been a stupid fool where you have been concerned, but he would perhaps not have succumbed to temptation if you had not pursued him so relentlessly,' he said. 'Can you imagine how my sister would feel to find out she has been usurped by a common little slut like you?'

Ally was incensed at his choice of words. 'If your sister was being a proper wife to him perhaps he wouldn't have strayed in the first place,' she threw back.

A tiny hammer of tension began beating beneath the dark stubble on his jaw next to his mouth. His coal-black eyes blazed with simmering anger, making her stomach suddenly contract in fear.

'You are like a bitch in heat,' he snarled at her. 'You will bed anyone, any time, for any cheap trinket thrown your way.'

Ally stiffened with fury. He was making her sister sound like an avaricious tramp. Although she didn't know all the details of Alex's life over the last twelve months, she wasn't going to allow Vittorio Vassallo to malign her twin without fighting back.

'Your brother-in-law is a two-timing creep,' she snipped at him. 'I pity his wife. I am sure I'm not the first woman he's had on the side.'

'You are right,' he said, surprising her with his candidness. 'Rocco is weak where beautiful women are concerned. His affair with you is not his first, and I dare say will not be his last.'

Ally tried to put some space between them, but the room was too small and he was too big. She could smell the lemon-based fragrance of his aftershave. It had been drifting towards her nostrils for the last few minutes, but she had been doing her best to ignore its alluring potency. And failing miserably. Her body was reacting to him in a way she had never thought possible. She was both frightened and attracted at the same time. He had a magnetic aura about him. He was the epitome of the successful businessman—wealth and prestige clung to him like a second skin—but she could see a glint of implacable ruthlessness in his eyes that secretly terrified her.

'You have caused rather an inopportune scandal for my brother-in-law and thereby my sister,' he said. 'The press are like baying hounds when it comes to anything to do with my family. I want to stop this current gossip in its tracks.'

Ally realigned her sagging posture. 'How do you propose to do that?' she asked.

He smiled a confident smile that irked her more than if he had called her a thousand opprobrious names. 'By diverting the attention from Rocco onto me,' he answered.

Ally knew she was repeating herself, but asked anyway, although her voice sounded uneven. 'H-how do you p-propose to do that?'

His dark-as-night eyes seared hers. 'You and I will conduct a very public affair of our own. I will pay you handsomely for your time, of course.'

She looked at him in stunned horror. 'An affair?' she choked. *'With you?'*

Vittorio had never had such a reaction from a woman before. It made him wonder if his brother-in-law had totally misread Mrs Alexandra Sharpe. Perhaps she was genuinely in love with Rocco. If so, it would make things even more complicated than they already were.

His sister Chiara was just a couple of weeks away from the danger zone of losing her baby, after struggling through a difficult pregnancy. If he could stall the gossip long enough to ensure the safe delivery of his niece or nephew it would be worth it. He did not care how much it would cost him. Besides, it wasn't going to be a real affair. He was determined not to sink so low as to take on the cast-offs of his brother-in-law, no matter how attractive they were. And Ally Sharpe was definitely attractive—but surprisingly not in the in-your-face way Rocco had described.

'It will not be a real affair,' he said. 'We will have to be seen in public and appear to be involved intimately. That is all I will require of you.'

Ally gritted her teeth at his contemptible proposal, everything in her repulsed by the way he was vicariously demeaning her sister. 'How much are you prepared to pay for my services as your pretend lover?' she asked.

His eyes bored into hers. 'How much do you normally charge for your services?'

Ally clenched her hands into fists in case she lifted one to his face in a slap, as she was sorely tempted to execute. She abhorred all forms of violence, but his condescending manner made her whole body shake with rage. 'I am *not* a whore,' she bit out. 'And nothing you say or do can make me one.' *Or my sister*, she tacked on mentally, her anger rising to an almost uncontrollable level.

His top lip lifted sardonically. 'I am prepared to pay you generously for two weeks of masquerading as my mistress,' he said. 'You will no doubt need clothes and other items fitting for the position. I have high standards, so I am quite willing to foot the bill for the length of the charade.'

Ally mentally calculated the cost of the clinic and the stack of outstanding bills she had come across in her sister's flat. It was a lot of money, and even though she was financially capable of covering most of it if she took out yet another short-term loan, she rationalised Vittorio Vassallo was a billionaire and had a lot to lose if 'she' didn't co-operate. Besides, it was because of his creep of a brother-in-law that her sister was now in the dreadful state she was in. It seemed fitting that Vassallo money should cover the cost of getting Alex back to normal, even though taking a single euro of it went against everything Ally believed in.

She met his gaze head-on and named a sum that would have stunned most people—but clearly not this man. He barely raised a brow as he looked down at her, his mocking smile grating on her already jangled nerves. 'You do put rather a high price on yourself, do you not?' he asked.

She gave him a pert look. 'I have always found you get what you pay for in life, Mr Vassallo. Or don't you follow that particular credo?'

'I do not believe in throwing good money after bad,' he returned. 'But if the amount you want is what will achieve the results I desire, then we will both be happy, *si*?'

Ally didn't roll her eyes, but she knew her acid tone delivered the same effect. 'Deliriously so.'

'Tell me, Mrs Sharpe,' he said, his hawk-like gaze still fixed on hers, 'do you feel even a tiny bit guilty about what you did to my car?'

She lifted her chin again. 'Actually, I don't feel guilty at all.'

His lips thinned in anger. 'Then I will endeavour to make you feel some measure of remorse,' he said. 'You are an unprincipled slut who wants someone else to foot your bills. I have met women like you before. You are after a sugar daddy—that is the term, is it not? '

'I want nothing of the sort,' she said through tight lips. 'I can pay my own way and fully intend to.'

'Then you will pay,' he said implacably. 'If you do not co-operate with my conditions you will not only be responsible for the damage to my car but for all the other things you have done to cause trouble for my family. If you think my brother-in-law is a push-over then think again in your dealings with me. You are not dealing with a man driven by his primal instincts but with a man driven by revenge.'

Ally felt the word reverberate through her slim body like a powerful earthquake, making her feel more vulnerable than she had ever felt in her life. Every part of her felt the tremors of terror as she realised she had just stepped into her sister's shoes, not knowing where in the world Alex had last been walking in them…

CHAPTER THREE

'PACK your bags,' Vittorio said. 'I will give you fifteen minutes to do so.'

Ally stared at him, her mouth opening and closing until she could find her voice. 'You want me to…to…come with you? *Now?*'

'But of course,' he answered smoothly. 'You are now my mistress—in the eyes of the press, at least. You will move into my *palazzo* overlooking the Villa Borghese immediately.'

Ally felt her heart begin to slam against her breastbone again in panic. 'But—'

'Do not argue with me, Mrs Sharpe.' He cut her off impatiently. 'I spoke with your landlord on the way in. He wants you out of here within a matter of days, otherwise he is threatening to take legal action. I took the liberty of paying him what you owed, so now I am the one you owe. You will do what I say or suffer the consequences of your actions. Staying in a *palazzo* for a couple of weeks will be much more pleasant than several months in a cramped cockroach-infested prison cell, *sì?*'

Ally tried to disguise her shudder of revulsion, but she was sure there was little that escaped his intelligent brown eyes. She could feel their dark intensity holding hers in a battle of wills she had no hope of winning. She knew all she had to do was show him the photo she had hidden earlier to bring an end to this madness right here and now. She could explain her sister's illness, hoping he would understand. But it was a risk she wasn't prepared to take—or at least not yet, not until she knew what sort of man Vittorio Vassallo was. For all she knew he would go ahead and press charges, and with the sort of affluence and connections he possessed she could imagine he would succeed in bringing about the revenge he spoke of earlier.

'If you don't mind I would rather stay in a hotel or something,' she said, desperately trying to quell her rising dread. 'We could still conduct our pretend affair. Moving in with you seems rather…er…extreme, don't you think?'

His jaw was set in a determined line. 'My brother-in-law might be content with conducting his secretive assignations in slum-like apartments or hotels, but I am afraid I am not prepared to give you such a convenient escape route. I know as soon as my back is turned you will disappear. I am not prepared to risk such a possibility. As my current mistress you will have a suite of rooms at my *palazzo* and be treated with the respect afforded to any other guest in my home. Besides, I wish to make it clear to everyone in my family that this is a real affair, even if in private it is not.'

Ally felt her stomach go hollow. 'H-how will you…? I mean, how will we convince people this is a *real* affair?'

His gaze contained that hint of mockery that had annoyed her from the first moment she had met him. 'You opened your legs for my brother-in-law, Mrs Sharpe,' he said, running his eyes over her in contempt. 'I am sure it will not stretch your capabilities to endure the occasional public kiss or hand-hold from me. That is all that will be required of you. I have no interest in anything else.'

Ally ran her tongue across her lips, and then wished she hadn't as his eyes dipped to her mouth, lingering there for a pulsing moment before he returned his dark enigmatic gaze to hers.

'So…any other questions?' he asked, as he ran a finger around the collar of his shirt as if he found it suddenly too tight.

'I think the press will find it strange to hear you call me Mrs Sharpe, don't you think?' she asked.

'You are right,' he said. 'Ally it will be from now on.'

The way he said her name made her skin feel ticklish, as if he had touched her all over with his fingertips in a light-as-air caress. 'W-what do you want me to call you?' she asked, feeling her colour begin to rise in spite of every effort on her part to remain unaffected by his disturbingly attractive presence.

He looked down at her for a moment or two, his eyes doing that drilling thing again. 'Vittorio will be fine. As I said, only my family and close friends call me Vito.'

'You don't consider any of your lovers as friends?'

'No, I do not,' he answered. 'I have found it impossible to maintain a platonic relationship with any of my ex-partners. Women do not seem to understand when it is time to move on.'

'And I suppose you are always the one who ends the relationship?' she said with a cynical look. 'I read an article about you recently which said you change mistresses as often as some people change their shirts.'

He returned her gaze without flinching. 'I admit I am easily bored,' he said. 'I do not see the point in dragging out a liaison which no longer holds any interest to me. It is better for both parties if things are terminated before anyone gets hurt.'

Ally flashed him a scornful glare. 'I hope one day you get your comeuppance, then,' she said. 'Men like you make me sick. You want your fun, but you don't want to commit to making a relationship work. It takes time and effort to make a relationship a good and fulfilling one.'

His eyes glinted with brewing anger. 'You are a fine one to talk, Mrs Sharpe. I believe you were the one who left your ex-husband, not the other way around?'

Ally wondered how much he knew of her sister's past, and how he had come by the information. Had Vittorio conducted his own investigation? It was a terrifying thought. There was so much she didn't know. The doctor had warned her not to stress her sister unnecessarily. The last thing she wanted to do was set off another breakdown by asking Alex probing questions about what had been going on over the last few weeks.

'I told you not to call me by that name,' she said, firing another fiery glare his way. 'And, even though it's really none of your business, I married young and regretted it from day one. I don't like discussing it. It distresses me to think of how impulsive I was back then.'

His eyes centred on hers. 'How old were you?' he asked.

Ally looked away. She hated lying to his face; it seemed much harder to do so with each lie she told. She felt as if she was constructing a precarious house of cards around herself; any minute a breath of truth would send them all toppling and expose her completely. 'I was eighteen,' she mumbled.

'Did your parents approve of the marriage?' he asked.

'No,' she said, unable to stop a little sigh escaping. 'Our...I mean my father left when I was a toddler, and my mother died when I was a few months off turning fifteen.'

'Who brought you up after your mother died?'

Ally found his questions deeply unsettling. She had spoken to so few people over the years about her and her sister's tragic background. Their various stints in foster care soon after the suicide of their mother had triggered the first episode of psychosis in her twin. It had been devastating to watch her rapid slide into insanity that had meant change after change of foster home as each carer found Alex's condition harder to cope with. Ally had fought hard to stay with her sister, which had made finding alternative placements all the more difficult.

Once they had turned sixteen she had left school to look after Alex full-time, gradually getting her back on her feet. It had been a struggle to go to night school to complete her education and then go on to do a degree—something Alex had never quite managed to achieve—but Ally felt she had done what needed to be done to provide for them both. Her job as a stock analyst for a European-based company director meant she could support them both financially during the periods her sister was out of work due to a relapse of her illness.

It had been almost three years since Ally had had to step in, which was why this episode was so upsetting as it seemed so out of the blue.

'Ally?'

She turned around to look at him, suddenly struck by the concerned way he was looking at her, as if he genuinely cared about what had happened to her in the past. 'I'm sorry...what did you ask me?' she said.

'I asked who looked after you after your mother died,' he said, his dark brown eyes momentarily losing their glittering hardness. 'Fourteen or even fifteen, particularly for a girl, is very young to be without an adult in her life. I have a niece who is close to that age. She adores her father, but I cannot imagine what she would do if she lost her mother. You had neither.'

Ally felt the burn of tears at the back of her eyes—tears she had forbidden herself from shedding for more than a decade. What was it about this man that affected her so? He was a playboy; he had admitted as much himself. He moved from one relationship to another like a child with a toy that no longer held any appeal. 'I was fostered out,' she said, lowering her eyes from his. 'Thank God there are still good people out there who open their homes for children in difficulties.'

Vittorio wondered why Rocco hadn't told him of his lover's tragic background, or if he had even known of it himself. It made sense that she craved security, given her young life had been disrupted so devastatingly, although a part of him wondered if it was all an act. What better way to garner sympathy than to construct a history of neglect and misery? Few people could resist a hard luck story; it drew on most people's heartstrings to think how tough others had it in life.

But there was something about the slim young woman before him that didn't quite add up. He couldn't quite put his finger on it. It was just a feeling he had. She was guarded around him, watching him from beneath the lashes of her brilliant blue eyes as if she was just waiting to be caught out. Although just for a moment he'd thought he had seen a film of moisture in her eyes before she had turned away, and it made him wonder if there was far more to Ally Sharpe than he had accounted for. He decided it might be in his interests to do a little covert digging to find out more about her background. Who knew what he might turn up?

'Do you need help to pack your things?' he asked after a little pause.

She gave him another one of her guarded looks. 'No…thank you. I haven't much with me. It won't take me more than a few minutes.'

Vittorio waited for her in the sitting room, his eyes sweeping the surfaces for anything that would give him a clue to who Alex Sharpe was. But there was nothing. No photos of loved ones, no personal belongings, no indication of where she had come from or where she was going. He knew she was Australian, although her accent was not as broad as some he had heard.

As was Rocco's way, he had only told Vittorio what he had wanted him to know of his relationship with Alex. Perhaps there was more to his brother-in-law's affair than he was letting on? All Rocco had told him was that she had come from Sydney and had spent a year working in London as an assistant in a budget fashion chainstore before moving to Rome. Apart from that he knew very little else. He knew his brother-in-law would not have taken the time to get to know her as a person; he would have been attracted to her physical attributes as any red-blooded man would be.

For God's sake, he was fiercely attracted to her himself! Being in the same room as her, smelling her feminine fragrance, seeing her cast her eyes downwards in that shy manner she had perfected to an art, had stirred his senses more than he would have thought possible. His blood had been boiling in his veins at standing so close to her just moments before. It had been unnervingly tempting to reach out and pull her into his arms and taste the sensual promise of her blood-red lips. He had never felt the urge to touch someone quite so intensely before. His relationships were always on his terms and his terms only. He started them and ended them as he saw fit. The thought of becoming involved with one of his brother-in-law's cast-offs was anathema to him. Apart from Chiara, Rocco had appalling taste when it came to women.

Thinking of his younger sister made him all the more determined to do whatever it took to keep this scandal out of the papers. Chiara had always been a little blind to Rocco's faults; she loved him so desperately she could not see how little he cared for her in return. They had only been married a year, and during that time Vittorio had been sickened to learn how many times Rocco had betrayed her. He just hoped that in time Chiara would feel strong enough to leave Rocco and build a better life for herself. But in the meantime there was not only his sister to worry about but the tiny baby she was carrying. If Alex Sharpe gave a damning interview to the press as she had threatened, it would devastate his sister and possibly jeopardise the baby's safe arrival.

He was *not* going to let that happen.

Ally carried two suitcases to the small sitting room, and had barely taken a step through the door when Vittorio strode over and took them both out of her hands. The brush of his long, strong fingers against hers sent her pulses suddenly soaring, the jolt of sexual energy from his body to hers something she was totally unprepared for. She snatched her hand away, her colour rising as she met his dark fathomless gaze.

'Is this all you want to take?' he asked.

She nodded, quickly lowering her eyes. 'The flat is a fully furnished one. I don't have much else but clothes.' *And the clothes and simple possessions of my sister in that second bag,* she thought, glancing at it nervously. It was starkly different from her conservative black one, with its simple green ribbon on the handle as an identifier. Alex's was bright yellow, and covered with colourful travel stickers, but if Vittorio Vassallo had noticed any difference he showed no sign of it on his face.

'My driver is waiting outside,' he informed her after a small pause. 'I would normally drive myself, but my car is in the workshop being resprayed.'

Ally followed him out of her sister's apartment on leaden legs, her heart doing crazy back-flips in her chest at the thought of what she had agreed to on Alex's behalf. When they were young they had often changed places, and usually very successfully. Not even their mother had been able to tell them apart at times. But somehow this was different.

It *felt* different.

It felt dangerous…

Vittorio exchanged a few words in Italian with his driver as he handed over the suitcases. Ally dearly wished she could understand what was being said, but from what she could make of the driver's expression when he looked at her he evidently realised he was in no position to argue with his employer over his choice of companion even if he wanted to. He clearly valued his job too much.

Once Vittorio was in the car beside her he leaned forward to close the panel that separated the driver from the passengers. 'Beppe does not approve of my being involved with a divorcée,' he said. 'Like a lot of people of his age and religious conviction, he is a little old-fashioned in that regard.'

Ally frowned as she tried to wriggle further away from those long, strong thighs of his that seemed to be taking up far too much room. 'You don't seem to me to be the type to be overly concerned about other people's opinions,' she said. 'If you were you would never have orchestrated this ridiculous charade in the first place.'

He stretched out one of his long arms along the back of the seat, his fingers so close to the nape of her neck that she felt every single hair stand to attention, as if anticipating his touch. She drew in a wobbly breath and sent out her tongue to remove the dry dust of panic from her lips.

'I have decided no one must know it is a charade,' he said, locking gazes with her. 'Apart from Rocco, of course.'

She sent him a worried glance. 'I don't have to see him, do I?'

He gave her a studied look. 'You will have to be seen with him amongst the rest of my family for our affair to be taken seriously. And you will have to be very careful you do not betray yourself by hankering after him like a lovesick fool.'

She turned her head and folded her arms crossly. 'I can assure you I will be doing no such thing.'

'I do not see why you should be so angry with him for breaking off your affair,' he said. 'You only slept with him—what was it?—two or three times? And he only did it because you threw yourself at him.'

'That's a lie!' Ally said, recalling her sister's tearful confession. 'He told me he loved me and was going to leave his wife for me.'

Vittorio's teeth ground together as he struggled to rein in his anger. 'You think he would leave his beautiful wife for a cheap little trollop like you? He used you just as you used him. A couple of quick tumbles in a sleazy hotel room, a handful of jewels and a wad of cash is usually how it goes with women like you, is it not?'

She glared back at him. 'Did he tell you he paid me?'

Vittorio held her dark blue gaze. 'No, but he did not need to—for you took the money yourself, did you not? You refused to go away. You wanted more than he was prepared to give. So you decided to make as much trouble for him as you could without giving a single thought as to how your behaviour would impact on other members of his family.'

Ally was at a loss to know what to say in response. She could imagine how desperately hurt Alex would have been to have been so cruelly shunted aside by the man she had fallen in love with—a man who had obviously lied to her from the start. It would have devastated her sister to find she had been betrayed in such a way, and while it didn't excuse her foolish behaviour in regard to Vittorio's car and the theft of the cash, Ally didn't feel it was fair that Alex had to shoulder all the blame while Rocco hid behind his wife's brother's broad back.

'I will tell the rest of my family and the press I have fallen for you,' Vittorio continued. 'I do not want anyone to suspect anything to the contrary in case it somehow gets back to my sister. She is enduring a difficult enough pregnancy as it is.'

Ally's eyes suddenly went wide. 'Rocco's wife is *pregnant?*' she gasped in shock.

His own eyes narrowed as he looked at her. 'Yes. Did he not tell you?'

She compressed her lips, wishing she had done so earlier, so those words wouldn't have come blurting out to raise that flag of suspicion in his astute brown gaze. 'I didn't even know he was married until after we…you know…got together.'

He made a sound of derision in his throat. 'You deceitful little tart.' He almost spat the words at her. 'You knew exactly what you were getting into. You chased him all the way from London. You have been hounding him for the last month, hoping to change his mind about keeping you in his bed.'

Ally was starting to put some pieces of the puzzle together in her head, and it didn't make a particularly attractive picture. From what she could make out Alex had had a fling with Rocco in London and fallen madly in love. Then, throwing in her job, had flown to Rome in the hope he would continue to see her. It went against everything she knew about her sister to think Alex would actively pursue a man whose wife was expecting a child. There must have been more to it than that. Someone was lying, and she was determined to find out the whole story before she revealed to Vittorio who she really was.

'I didn't know about his wife's pregnancy,' she said, reasonably confident she was speaking for her twin. 'He never once mentioned it.'

He suddenly grasped her chin between two strong fingers, forcing her gaze to meet his. 'I do not believe you,' he ground out. 'My brother-in-law told me how devious you are, how conniving you can be when you want something you cannot have.'

Ally glared at him venomously. 'If you put your hands on me again I will scratch your arrogant face until even your cad of a brother-in-law doesn't recognise you.'

His smile was deliberately taunting as he released her. 'You have quite a spirit,' he observed musingly. 'It needs to be tamed, of course, but we have two weeks in which to do so. I am confident I can get you eating out of my hand, given the right inducement.'

She sent him a scathing look. 'You would need more than two weeks to tame me, you arrogant bastard. You are exactly the sort of man I abhor. You see women as objects to titillate your every need. You lure them in and then cast them aside as if they mean nothing to you. You disgust me. My flesh crawls at the thought of you touching me.'

'And yet you enjoyed the attentions of my brother-in-law, a man who belongs to someone else?'

Ally could hear the disgust in his tone, and turned her head to look out of the window so she didn't have to see it on his face. It upset her more than she wanted it to. Having an affair with a married man was a mistake any woman could make if the man didn't reveal his marital status early in the piece, but what if her sister *had* eventually known about Rocco's wife's pregnancy?

It worried her that Alex might have been unstable enough to continue the affair regardless. She had been off her medication for weeks, maybe even longer. That in itself was a recipe for disaster. She had witnessed her sister's rapid mood swings before. Life was like an out-of-control rollercoaster when Alex was not properly medicated. It was such a delicate balancing act, getting the right levels, making sure her sister stayed on her medication regime and avoided all the triggers that would cause a relapse.

'But you are not my brother-in-law's mistress now,' he said. 'To all intents and purposes you are mine. Every step you take from this moment on will be documented by the press. If you put even one foot wrong the prison cell I was talking about will become a cold, hard reality. Do not think I will not do it, for I can and I will if I feel it is necessary.'

Ally secretly admired his loyalty to his brother-in-law and pregnant sister. It reminded her of her own devotion to Alex. She almost wished she could tell him so, but current circumstances prevented it. Although he was undoubtedly a playboy, he seemed so much more principled than his cowardly brother-in-law.

The car pulled into a leafy street close to the Villa Borghese. The driver was out of the car and dealing with the suitcases before Ally could even unfold her trembling legs from the vehicle.

She looked up at the impressive building; it was a seven-teenth-century *palazzo*, with several sun-drenched terraces that made the most of the view over the city and the green oasis that housed so many of the tourist attractions she had read about in her travel guide.

The warm air carried a seductive hint of honeysuckle and star jasmine as she walked up the steps with Vittorio's palm beneath her elbow, the touch of his flesh against hers sending little jolts of electricity up and down her arm.

'I have cleared my diary for the next few days,' he said as they entered the building. 'We will spend as much time as possible together in order to send a very clear message to the press that they got it wrong when they cited you as Rocco's lover. It happens occasionally, as we are very similar in looks and are the same age. We could almost be taken for twins.'

Ally physically stumbled on the *palazzo* steps as he mentioned the word. She looked up at him, to see if he had noticed anything untoward, but he was already speaking to someone who appeared to be some sort of senior housekeeper. She couldn't follow the staccato Italian, but she caught one or two words that seemed to suggest Vittorio's household staff were not generally used to accommodating his various mistresses. The looks she was receiving seemed to confirm it. She was apparently in a class of her own, being allowed access to his private domain. She wasn't sure what to make of that. Although it made sense he would want everyone to assume she was his current lady-love, and moving into his *palazzo* was certainly a confirmation to the press that she was being treated unlike any other woman he had been involved with previously.

'You have been assigned the suite of rooms next to mine,' Vittorio said. 'There is an adjoining door between the bed-rooms, but you can lock it on your side if you should feel the need to do so.'

Ally couldn't help curling her lip at him. 'You surely don't think I would be tempted to crawl into *your* bed, do you?'

His eyes communicated his arrogant disdain. 'You would be turned away if you did,' he said in a harsh undertone. 'I have no interest whatsoever in pursuing any sort of relationship with you. You are exactly the sort of woman I make every effort to avoid. You are clingy and dependent, intent on finding yourself a benevolent fool who will indulge your every whim.'

Ally was sure his bruising tirade wasn't over, but the appearance of yet another staff member put an abrupt end to it.

A demure young woman carrying a vase of summer roses smiled shyly, and in halting English asked if Ally would like to be shown her room.

'That would be lovely, thank you,' Ally said, without bothering to seek Vittorio's approval. She was exhausted, and could think of nothing better than a few minutes on her own to gather her scattered thoughts.

The suite the girl called Ghita led her into was luxuriously appointed beyond anything Ally had ever experienced. The floors were of polished Italian marble, covered here and there with ankle-deep rugs, and the windows were full length, festooned with voluminous silk curtains, and overlooked massive gardens awash with colourful blooms similar to the fragrant ones the young girl had just placed on the bedside table.

'Would you like me to pour you a cool drink?' Ghita asked. 'It is very hot today, *sì*?'

Ally smiled, instantly relaxing in the atmosphere of the girl's open friendliness. 'Yes, it is. I'm not used to it yet. I guess it will take a few more days to acclimatise. It was still winter when I left home.'

It was only when Ghita gave her a confused look that Ally realised her little slip. 'I—I m-mean it was much cooler in London than here,' she amended quickly.

'*Sì*,' Ghita said, smiling again. 'I have not been to England. I have heard it rains a lot there, yes?'

'Yes,' Ally said, surreptitiously letting out a relieved sigh. 'It does.'

'Signor Vassallo is very nice, is he not?' Ghita said. 'I think it very funny how the paparazzi got it wrong—you know, about you being Signor Rocco's lover.'

'Yes…yes, it was highly…er…amusing…' Ally said weakly, searching around for her handbag without success. Had she left it in the car, or was it with the rest of her things? It had been on the floor of the car at her feet. Her mind was so rattled and her head was starting to pound so sickeningly she couldn't remember whether she had brought it upstairs or not. She thought of the money stashed inside it and wished she could ask Alex what she had been doing with it. Had she stolen it from Rocco Montano, as Vittorio had said? Her sister might be a little unpredictable at times, but Ally was sure Alex would never take something that wasn't hers.

'Ghita, do you think you could bring me my handbag?' she asked. 'I think I must have left it in the car, or on one of the tables in the foyer. I have the beginnings of a headache, and I have some painkillers that will ease it if I take them in time.'

'*Sì*,' Ghita said. 'I will see to it straight away.'

The young girl came back a few moments later with Ally's bag and handed it to her.

'Anyway, the press are *stupido*,' she prattled on as she poured a tall glass of iced water from a jug on a side table. 'They know nothing about anything. Everyone knows they make things up to sell papers and magazines.'

'Oh, really?' Ally asked absently as she took the glass from the girl and swallowed two pills from her bag.

'Why would you damage Signor Vassallo's car if you were Rocco's lover?' Ghita asked. 'It does not make sense. It was a lovers' tiff, no? You were angry at Signor Vittorio for not publicly acknowledging you. So what if you have been married before? It is the twenty-first century, *sì*? But he has openly presented you now, and all is well, is it not? You are here in his *palazzo*. No other woman has ever had that privilege. It will be fun. Like a *celebrazione*, no?'

Ally had never felt less like celebrating in her life, but she smiled back at the young girl regardless. 'Yes,' she said, her stomach tying itself into knots. 'I'm sure it will be heaps of fun.'

CHAPTER FOUR

ALLY whooshed out an exhausted breath once the young house-maid had left. She sank onto one of the deeply cushioned sofas and, laying back her head, closed her eyes, trying to allow the pills to do their job and ease the vice-like tension across her brow.

She had never been in such an awkward position before. She felt as if she was betraying every principle she had clung to all of her life. Honesty and openness had been tossed aside for subter-fuge and mendacity. How long could she maintain this appallingly dangerous charade? What if she had to meet her twin's lover face to face? Would *he* see the swap for what it was? After all, he had been her sister's lover. The physical intimacy they had shared, even if it had only been on a few occasions, would surely give him an edge Vittorio did not have, having only met her the once.

Even thinking about Vittorio Vassallo set her nerves jumping all over the place. He was going to be sleeping on the other side of that door—the door that she had not yet locked. What if he took it upon himself and came in to claim his mock mistress? She wouldn't put it past him. She had seen the attraction in his black-as-night gaze every time it rested on her, reluctant as it was. He was fighting it just as much as she was, but for totally differ-ent reasons. He would think it beneath himself to sample his brother-in-law's leftovers, but she had much more to lose—her virginity, for one thing. Even though she was twenty-five years old, she had never taken a lover. There had been plenty of op-portunities, but her natural reserve had made her cautious around men. And her responsibilities towards her twin had made it almost impossible at times to have a life of her own. It had only been during the last year or so that she had felt an easing of the burden, and even so it had all blown up in her face yet again.

She clenched her hands in determination. She *had* to get Alex through this. If it took every ounce of courage, every atom of her being, to see her sister come out the other side in full health again it would be worth it.

There was a knock at the door, and, hoping it was the cheerful little Ghita, with fresh water for the jug Ally had almost drained, she rose to answer it.

Vittorio's tall figure stooped as he entered the room, his eyes immediately going to the door that separated his room from hers. 'I notice you have not locked the door,' he commented, turning back to look at her. 'What does that mean, I wonder? Is it that you trust me to keep my side of the bargain, or are you hoping I will change my mind and be tempted to sample you for myself, as Rocco has done?'

'I wouldn't sleep with you if you paid me a king's ransom,' she spat back venomously.

'You slept with my brother-in-law for what you could get out of him,' he said. 'If money and notoriety is what you want then I can give you much more of both than Rocco ever could.'

Her mouth tightened as she held his challenging look. 'I told you why I slept with him, and it had nothing to do with money.'

'Ah, yes.' His mocking smile was back. 'You fell in love with him. Or perhaps it was the size of his wallet, no? I am sure you checked that out before you—' he made the finger sign of quotation marks in the air '—"lost your heart" to him.'

She frowned at him. 'You don't think it's possible for someone to fall in love not knowing anything about the other person?' she asked. 'What about instant chemistry? Or connecting on some other level, such as intellectually or spiritually?'

His eyes glinted at her. 'You are as convincing as Rocco warned. He said you had ways and means about you that would make any man crazy with lust for you.'

She upped her chin, her brilliant blue eyes challenging him.

'But not you, Mr Vittorio-Never-Makes-an-Error-of-Judgement-Vassallo? Right?'

His eyes locked with hers. 'How much would you want to make this affair a real one?'

She looked at him as if he had just asked her to straighten the Tower of Pisa with one fingertip. *'What did you say?'* Her voice came out like a squeak.

He stepped up close to her, one of his hands threading through the silk of her silver-blonde hair, coiling it around his fingers, tethering her to him. 'How much to be my mistress?' he asked again, softly this time, smoulderingly, seductively.

Ally's eyes went wide with both apprehension and attraction. She could barely make sense of it. One part of her wanted to slap that arrogantly confident look off his too handsome face. The other part of her—the part she didn't even recognise as herself—wanted to wind her arms around his neck and bring that sensual mouth down to hers. She could feel the seductive pull of his inscrutable dark gaze as it warred with hers, and she could see the flare of his pupils signalling the desire he was no longer bothering to conceal. The thought of him possessing her intimately made her knees sag and her legs go weak. She could feel her inner body beginning to pulse with an ache for fulfilment she instinctively knew he would be more than capable of satisfying. She felt it in his touch; she breathed it in his male scent. The power and potency of him was making her whole body leap to fervent life.

'I am a very rich man, Ally,' he said into the erotically charged silence. 'What is it you want? Diamonds? An apartment? An all-expenses-paid holiday to somewhere exotic?'

Ally moistened her lips, wondering what he would say if she told him what she really wanted. She wanted her sister to be well most of all—and she would *do* anything, and *give* anything to bring that about.

But for herself personally? That was simple. It was what most women wanted. Ally wanted to be loved, to be swept off her feet and adored by a man who would remain faithful to her, supporting her through all of life's ups and downs. And she wanted to have children, so she could experience the stability of a loving family unit and make up for all she and Alex had missed out on in the past.

'I want security,' she said in the end, taking the middle ground. 'It is how women are made. It's in our genetic code. We choose partners on the basis of how good a provider they can be. There is nothing sinister or avaricious about it. It's just the way things are.'

His mouth slanted in a smile as he slowly unwound her hair from his fingers. 'So you are making a science out of seduction, no?'

Ally pursed her lips at him, trying not to shiver in reaction as each hair on her head responded to his touch. 'I'm not trying to seduce you, Vittorio,' she said. 'I am trying to be sensible about this…this unusual situation we are in.'

His charcoal eyes bored into hers. 'It is, as you say, unusual—but that does not mean it cannot be mutually satisfying,' he said. 'You apparently made the mistake of falling for a married man. I dare say a lot of women have done so many times before, and no doubt very many will continue to do so in the future. But I am not married, and you are now free, so why not explore the possibilities?'

'W-what do you mean by p-possibilities?' she asked, stumbling over her words as he cupped the nape of her neck with the warmth of his palm.

His gaze went to her mouth. 'Do I need to spell it out for you, Ally?'

Her throat moved up and down as his gaze locked on hers. 'I'm not ready for…for any…er…entanglements…' she said.

'Do not tell me you still have hankerings after Rocco?' he asked as his index finger began a slow caress from the shell of her ear right to the corner of her mouth.

Ally gave a mental gulp as he stopped just short of her tingling, quivering lips. 'N-no, this is not about Rocco,' she said. 'I care nothing for him.'

He hooked one brow upwards, his dark eyes still watching her intently. 'Nothing at all, eh?'

She gave her head a little shake. 'No…he means nothing to me…er…now.'

He studied her features in silence for a moment or two before saying, 'I will leave you to prepare for our first public outing this evening. I have already phoned my older sister Justina and her husband, and told them of our affair. They will accept you as my current love interest—you will have no need to feel uncomfortable around them if you happen to meet them over the next few days. They believe, as I had hoped, that the press made a stupid mistake.'

'What about Rocco? Have you told him about us?' Ally asked.

'Yes, but he was not happy about my solution to the problem,' he said, his dark, mysterious gaze piercing as it held hers. 'I found that intriguing, considering he begged me to do something about you hassling him.'

Ally sent her tongue out to moisten her lips. 'Perhaps your brother-in-law hasn't told you everything that went on between us? Have you considered that?'

'I am looking into it from all angles, so to speak, in case one or both of you is not being up-front and honest with me,' he said with another penetrating look. 'But I think I already know who is lying. It is so obvious, is it not?'

Ally felt her nerves start to fray at the edges at his cat-and-mouse tactics. 'I will not be toyed with by you as I was by your cowardly brother-in-law,' she said tightly. 'I am not some cheap tart who can be bought and then thrown away when you're finished with me. I'm telling you now if I *was* really involved with you I would *not* go away without a fight.'

He moved forward again, before she could counteract it, and tipped up her chin with his hard fingers, his eyes clashing with hers. 'Then you have just met your match, Ally Sharpe,' he said with a smouldering look. 'For I like nothing better than a showdown, and this one I can feel in my blood is going to end up with us in bed.'

Ally pulled out of his hold and glared up at him. 'Get out!' she shrieked. 'Get out of here you bast—'

He put his hand over her mouth, blocking the rest of her words. 'Do not shout at me, *cara*,' he said in an infuriatingly calm tone. 'The household staff will think we are not as in love as we claim to be.'

Ally tried to say *I hate you* against the firm pressure of his palm, but it came out muffled. So instead she sank her teeth into the pad of his thumb, hard enough to break the skin. He put her from him with a muttered curse, his mouth covering the place where hers had been. There was something disconcertingly intimate about the action; his mouth was now in contact with traces of her saliva.

She took a step backwards, shocked at her behaviour, ashamed by how she was reacting to him. 'I—I'm sorry,' she said, her colour rising. 'Are you…are you OK?'

He wrapped his thumb in his handkerchief before he met her anxious gaze. 'It is nothing—just a scratch.'

She stepped forward and took his hand, carefully unwrapping the makeshift bandage and looking at the imprint of her teeth on his skin.

She looked up at him, his hand still cradled in hers. 'Please forgive me. I can't believe I just did that. I'm not normally the type of person to lose control like that.'

His dark eyes seemed to be particularly intent as they held hers. 'Not according to my brother-in-law. And do not forget I have photographs of you acting very much out of control.'

Ally bit her bottom lip as she let his hand go. 'I'm not really myself right now,' she said with unintentional irony. 'I have been having some problems lately…'

'What sort of problems?'

'Emotional stuff,' she said, lowering her gaze a fraction. 'I'll be fine now. I've finally accepted Rocco is not available. I was naïve to get involved with him. I should have seen the signs. I'm hopeless at reading people—married men in particular. Some are just flirting for the sake of it. I should have left him alone, but I became a little obsessed. I feel embarrassed thinking about it now. It was so out of character and immature of me.'

'It is of no importance now,' he said. 'We have resolved the situation rather cleverly, have we not? In two weeks it will all be over. You can go back to London or Australia and resume your former life.'

'Yes…' Ally said, thinking longingly of her neat, ordered life back at home. She didn't want to think about how boring and empty it seemed in comparison. Doing so made the last few hours seem like a hair-raising rollercoaster of emotion—emotion she had never thought herself capable of feeling.

Vittorio moved to the door. 'I will see you downstairs at seven. I will send Ghita up to show you the way.'

Ally watched as the door closed behind him. She felt as if she was trapped inside with all her lies, each one she had told circling above her head like a hornet waiting to strike.

She gave a little shiver and turned away—only to confront the door that connected Vittorio's sleeping quarters with hers. She drew in a prickly breath and walked across the cloud-soft rug. She lifted her hand to turn the key, but before she had even placed her fingers on the key she heard the sound of the door being locked from the other side. Her hand fell back by her side, her breathing shallow and uneven as she thought about what had motivated Vittorio to lock the door himself.

Was it because he didn't trust her? Or, even more alarming, was it because he didn't trust himself?

Ally took her mobile into the bathroom with her and called her sister, only to be told by one of the clinic staff that Alex was having a particularly bad time of it and had had to be heavily sedated again.

'I am afraid she began self-mutilating,' the psychiatric nurse informed her soberly. 'Somehow she found something sharp. The doctor has changed the dosage of her medication, so she should be feeling better in a day or two. I will tell her you called.'

Ally felt her stomach clench in anguish. 'Do you think I should come straight there as soon as I can get a train or a flight?' she asked.

'No, it is better for us to deal with her. Sometimes visits by family members can make things harder in the early stages of rehabilitation. We have a wonderful therapist who is assigned to Alex. She is confident she can bring your sister back to full health. Try not to be too concerned—she is in very good hands. We just have to be patient until she is stabilised.'

In spite of the clinic nurse's assurances, Ally felt sick with worry as she closed the face of her phone. But she had other things to be concerned about besides her sister's health. In less than two hours she had to meet the press in her role as Vittorio Vassallo's mistress. How on earth would she maintain her composure if he decided to kiss her, as she was almost certain he had intended to do earlier? Her lips were still buzzing from that feather-light touch that had come so tantalisingly close to her mouth.

She wasn't used to men like Vittorio Vassallo. He was too powerful, too arragantly male, too disturbingly attractive, and way too clever to be outwitted by someone as hopelessly inadequate as her. She was living on a razor edge; every moment was fraught with the possibility of being exposed. She realised she would have to tread even more carefully now. The last thing she needed was to fall in love with Vittorio Vassallo. Not only was he way out of her league, since the moment they had met she had done nothing but deceive him...

After a short rest Ally had a cool shower—only to come out of the *en suite* bathroom and find Ghita had unpacked her suitcase. She was now trying to unlock Alex's case, fortunately without success.

'It's all right,' Ally said, securing the towel around her breasts. 'I don't need that one unpacked.'

The young housemaid looked at her in surprise. 'But Signor Vassallo told me to unpack all of your things. I must do as he says or I might lose my job.'

Ally took the case and, sliding open the large wall-to-wall wardrobe, shoved it in and closed the door again. 'There,' she said, turning to smile at the girl. 'Now he'll never know. It can be our little secret.'

Ghita still looked worried. 'You do not have much with you,' she said. 'I pressed your clothes while you were in the bathroom, and it did not take me long. You only have one evening dress in that bag. You will need more than that if you are to live with Signor Vassallo.'

Ally unwound the towel she had turban-like on her head, keeping her gaze averted from Ghita's curious one. 'I don't think I will be staying here all that long. I am sure you have seen many of his women-friends come and go before. I'm surprised he hasn't fitted a revolving door on his bedroom.'

Ghita giggled. 'He is...I do not know how to say it in English...*alesato facilmente*.'

Ally turned to look at her blankly. 'I'm sorry, I don't understand.'

Ghita's brow wrinkled as she searched for an alternative. 'He is *agitato*.'

'Agitated? Restless?'

The young housemaid smiled. 'That is it! Restless and easily bored. You are helping me so much with my English. I have not studied as hard as I should. I left school too early—but I had to as my mother became ill. She is better now, but I did not want to go back to school.'

'I think you speak very well indeed,' Ally said.

'*Grazie*, Signora Sharpe,' Ghita said, blushing slightly.

'Please call me Ally,' Ally insisted. 'I hate being addressed by my married name.'

'What is your maiden name?' Ghita asked.

'Benton,' Ally said.

'That is a nice name.'

'Thank you...I mean *grazie*, Ghita.'

Ghita grinned. 'You will be speaking Italian like a native in no time.'

'I don't think I will be here long enough to pick up more than one or two phrases,' Ally said as she selected underwear from where Ghita had neatly stored it in the wardrobe.

'It is true Signor Vassallo does not settle very long with anyone, but you are the first he has brought here to his *palazzo*,' Ghita said. 'My mother says he is looking for the perfect woman—but who is perfect? There is no such thing. Women are human, *sì*?'

'Yes, very much so,' Ally agreed.

'Do you need help getting dressed?' Ghita asked.

'No, thank you, Ghita, I can manage. As you say, I only have the one dress, and it won't take me long to dry my hair and put on some make-up.'

'I am sure Signor Vassallo will buy you many beautiful things while you are with him. He is very generous with his lovers.' Ghita smiled wistfully. 'I am sure he is *magnifico* in the bedroom, no?'

'I really wouldn't know about—' Ally began, quite flustered.

Realising she might have overstepped the mark, Ghita sheepishly returned to her work.

Ally was relieved when the young girl left her to dress in peace. She didn't want to hear about Vittorio's past lovers or his prowess in bed. She didn't want to even *think* about him with another woman. In fact she didn't want to think about him at all—but that was going to be impossible with whatever he had planned for her for the next two weeks, living with him in his *palazzo* under the watchful eye of the media. How on earth was she going to bear it?

Vittorio was standing looking out of the west-facing terrace windows when Ghita led Ally into the room. He turned and felt a shockwave of red-hot desire pulse through him at the vision of her standing there, so elegantly tall in her heels, her slim body perfectly showcased in a pastel blue satin cocktail dress that clung lovingly to every delightful curve of her body. Her face was delicately made up, neither too little nor too much, just enough to bring out the unusual deep blue of her eyes and the creamy perfection of her skin.

Her appearance confirmed everything he had learned in a few choice phone calls a few minutes ago. He wanted to be angry at her, but instead he felt as if she had unlocked his hardened heart in a way he had never imagined possible. It would perhaps be mean of him to allow her to continue her charade for a little longer, but he found her act so delightfully charming now some of the pieces of the puzzle had slipped into place. She was so endearingly naïve, so devoted to keeping her façade in place, she had no idea how many clues she was dropping without realising it. Leaving her handbag in the car had been one of them. What he had found inside had confirmed his suspicions. But he wanted to find out a little more before he showed her his hand.

'*Tesore mio,*' he said, moving towards her to hook her right arm through his left one. 'You look absolutely stunning. I almost wish we were not going out to dine after all. I would much prefer to spend the evening alone with you here. I am sure we would find plenty to do to entertain ourselves, *si*?'

Ally felt her face begin to flush as his fingers stroked the bare skin of her arm in a sensual movement that sent the nerves beneath into a mad frenzy. She wished she could step out of his hold, but with the young housemaid looking on with beaming approval Ally knew she was momentarily trapped.

'I have made a reservation at a favourite restaurant of mine,' he said, as he led her to where his driver was waiting outside. 'It is up a lane close to one of Rome's most famous tourist spots—the Trevi Fountain. Have you thrown a coin into it yet?'

'No, not yet,' Ally said, her flesh tingling where his hand was touching her on the arm. 'But I've heard about the legend. If you throw a coin over your shoulder into the fountain it means you will some day return to Rome.'

'Ah, yes, but there are three parts to the legend. The second and third are not so commonly known,' he said as he settled her into the car.

'What are they?' she asked. His fingers brushed against hers as he pulled down the seat belt and handed it to her.

His eyes were inscrutably dark as they meshed with hers. 'One coin is, as you say, a return to Rome. However, if you throw in two it means you will fall in love with an Italian, and three coins means you will marry one.'

Ally studied his face; something in his tone troubled her. There was a glint of devilry in his gaze, as if he was toying with her like a predator with its targeted prey before the final fatal pounce.

She turned her head and looked fixedly out of the window as the late-evening sun cast golden beams across the green expanse of the Villa Borghese as they drove past. 'I couldn't think of anything worse than marrying an Italian man,' she said. 'As far as I can see they are not to be trusted.'

'I was thinking the very same thing about Australian women,' he returned smoothly.

She swivelled back to look at him, her heart beating irregularly in her chest. 'W-what makes you say that?'

'You will have to stop looking at me like that, Ally,' he said. 'We are supposed to be madly in love, remember? I cannot have you looking daggers at me all the time, otherwise our little charade will be seen for what it is.'

'I think I should warn you right here and now I'm not a very good actor,' she said in a petulant tone. 'I was dropped from the school play when I was ten years old for not being convincing enough as a bumble bee.'

The sudden white slash of his enigmatic smile set her heart on yet another rollercoaster ride. 'I think you will do very well indeed,' he said. 'You were obviously miscast way back then, but this role is perfect for you. You were made for it, *sì*?'

Ally didn't answer. She turned to look at the passing scenery, with her frantically flying thoughts flapping their wings of panic inside her head. Had he somehow guessed she wasn't who she had said she was? But if he had guessed why didn't he say so? Why prolong her agony? Why not lay his cards on the table so they both knew where they stood? What possible motive could he have for allowing her to continue what could only be described as her increasingly farcical deception?

The driver let them out in a narrow cobblestoned lane a short distance from the Trevi Fountain, and within moments of exiting the car the assembled press surged forward, along with a massive tourist crowd, as if they had automatically sensed someone notable had arrived. Cameras flashed and the rapid fire of Italian assaulted Ally's ears like clanging bells as each member of the paparazzi vied for the best shot.

Ally tried to look as if she was used to such attention, but the press of hot bodies unnerved her. To avoid them she leaned into Vittorio's solid frame for protection. She felt the warmth of his palm in the small of her back, making the nerves beneath her skin flutter in reaction and her legs to feel woolly and useless.

She listened as the questions flew back and forth, but although she recognised a few words here and there she was really at a loss as to what was being said—until a young female journalist with a Scottish accent addressed Vittorio in English.

'Mr Vassallo, a rumour has been going around that you are

covering up for your brother-in-law's affair with Mrs Sharpe by pretending to be involved with her yourself. Do you have any comment to make about that?'

Ally felt Vittorio's arm around her waist tighten slightly. 'Yes, I do,' he said with an urbane smile. 'Your people have most definitely got it wrong. This is not a cover-up. Ally Sharpe is not just my current lover but my fiancée. She has already moved into my *palazzo*, and we plan to marry in a matter of weeks.'

CHAPTER FIVE

ALTHOUGH it was a relief to be finally shepherded into the restaurant a few moments later, the press barred from entry by the stern reprimand of the owner, Ally's heart-rate was still jumping all over the place at Vittorio's comment to the journalist.

'I have a special table prepared for you at the back,' the restaurant owner said to Vittorio. 'You will not be disturbed, I will see to it personally.'

He was as good as his word for, although the main part of the restaurant was soon filled to capacity, apart from the waiter assigned to them they saw no one, as fresh bread and olive oil was brought to the table along with the menu and wine list.

'How do you feel about having your photo splashed across tomorrow's papers and all the European gossip magazines?' Vittorio asked, once the wine he had chosen had been poured for them.

Ally compressed her lips, her fingers fiddling with the stem of her glass in an abstracted manner. 'I'm not keen on the idea, but I suppose if it achieves the aim it will be worth it. Don't you think the fiancée comment you made was a little over the top?'

'I thought your intention was to find yourself a rich husband?' he said, reaching for his glass and taking a sip, all without releasing her gaze from the magnetism of his.

A small frown tugged at her forehead. 'You didn't mean it…did you? I mean, you wouldn't take things that far…*would you*?'

He smiled an unreadable smile. 'You do not find me an attractive prospect as a husband?'

She ran her tongue over her lips in an agitated gesture. 'It's not that… It's just you could marry anyone you liked. Why would you tie yourself to someone like me given my…er…past? Isn't that taking family responsibility to extremes? Surely your brother-in-law and even your sister wouldn't expect it of you?'

'I do not make a habit of seeking my brother-in-law's approval for my actions,' he said. 'I am quite enjoying your company, in spite of what he said about you. I think we could make quite a match of it actually. Besides…' His dark gaze ran over her like a hot licking flame as he added sultrily, 'I would hate to think of all that sexual chemistry that pulses between us going to waste.'

Ally looked at him in heart-thudding alarm. 'Y-you're teasing me. You have to be. You c-couldn't possibly want to take things that far!'

His expression remained frustratingly unreadable. 'You know, you really are a very intriguing young woman,' he said. 'I thought your whole intention was to find yourself a sugar daddy. Does the thought of marrying a billionaire no longer hold appeal?'

'I don't like the thought of being married to anyone who isn't in love with me,' she said, chewing her lip as she tried to make sense of this latest development. What was he doing, for God's sake? Testing to see if she would take the bait her sister might have in her place?

'Was that your mistake the first time?' he asked into the silence.

'I…' She looked away from his piercing gaze. 'I'm a completely different person now. What I wanted back then is not what I want now.'

'Another thing I have observed about you that runs against what Rocco told me is that you do not really enjoy being the centre of attention,' he said. 'I sometimes feel as if he completely misread you. He described you as an out-and-out extrovert, flirtatious and vivacious, the life of the party. But that is not the real you, is it? You hate crowds. I saw the way you reacted just then. I could feel the tension in your body. You could not wait to get away. How could Rocco have got it so wrong about you?'

She lifted her eyes to his, wondering if there was more behind his comment than he was letting on. 'I'm sure I don't need to tell you Rocco is not the sort of person to be interested in getting to know someone deeply. To put it crudely, he was only interested in getting himself laid.'

'Which you agreed to within hours of meeting him—or so he told me.'

'And do you believe everything your brother-in-law tells you?' she asked with a pointed look.

'I am not unaware of Rocco's limitations,' he said, releasing a small sigh as he replaced his glass on the table. 'While I admire him in a professional capacity, he is not the person I would have chosen to marry my younger sister. I tried to warn her about him, but you know what young girls are like. They do not like being told what to do. Of course it did not help that she had had a crush on him for years. Chiara has been emotionally vulnerable since our parents died in a road accident when she was a teenager. I blame myself for not being there for her. I was studying abroad at the time, at Cambridge in England, and our older sister Justina was married and living in Athens. Chiara was all alone. I will never forget that phone call…'

He paused for a moment and picked up his glass, studying the contents before adding, as his eyes met hers, 'I am probably boring you with all this. I do not normally share such intimate information with just anyone. You are a good listener, Ally. That is something else Rocco neglected to tell me about you.'

Ally was so close to telling him the truth she had to bite her tongue. He seemed so genuine, so sincere, but how could she be sure?

'I told you what happened between your brother-in-law and I was a mistake,' she said, lowering her eyes once more. 'If I could have avoided all of this I would have, but Rocco lied to me. If he had told me he was married I would have never dreamt of getting involved with him.'

'When exactly did he tell you he was married?'

She tried to recall what her twin had said. 'Um…I think it was on our last date.'

'Where was that?'

. She felt her heart flap in her chest like a stranded fish. 'In London…'

'Whereabouts in London?' he asked.

She frowned in frustration. 'What does it matter where it was? A lie is a lie, no matter where it is delivered.'

'That is true,' he agreed. 'But it is important for me to know what happened between you and when. I thought it might be beneficial to get your angle and weigh things up in my mind.'

'So you can decide who is more credible?' she asked, with a cynical twist to her mouth.

He looked at her steadily for a lengthy pause, the dark intensity of his gaze unravelling her more than he could have imagined as she sat rigidly before him, every muscle in her face twitching under the tight control she was trying to maintain on her features. Her pulse was racing, her skin breaking out in a fine sweat, and her stomach was feeling as if a giant hole had been carved into it with a sharp implement.

'As I said before, the picture he painted of you does not quite fit the frame I see before me now,' he said, raising his glass to his lips again. 'I wonder why that is?'

Ally swallowed against the restriction in her throat. 'Your brother-in-law is hardly someone I'd be putting my money on to trust,' she said. 'He openly cheated on his pregnant wife. What sort of man does that?'

'What sort of woman pursues such a man, in spite of what she knows of his marital status?' he tossed back.

Ally clenched her fists under the table. 'Do you have any idea what it's like for women of today?' she asked. 'Some men these days can be *so* selfish. They want their cake and they want it with whoever can provide it. They don't want to commit, they don't want to stay in for the long haul. Women don't have the luxury of a seemingly endless timeline. Finding a suitable mate and settling down loom large in a woman's mind—even a career-driven woman such as me.'

He hooked one dark brow upwards as he set his glass back down on the crisp white tablecloth. 'You call working as a sales assistant in a budget fashion chainstore a career?' he asked.

Ally gave herself a mental kick and hoped he couldn't see how on edge she was under his tight scrutiny. 'I believe it's important to understand any business from the ground up. I don't see how cleaning the bathrooms or serving customers is any less important than being a company CEO. If you don't have good, dedicated staff representing your business you don't have a business, as far as I'm concerned.'

'I could not agree with you more,' he said. 'That is why I am so concerned about my brother-in-law's behaviour, and why I am prepared to go to such extremes to cover it up. Word of mouth is everything in finance. Glossy advertisements do not cut it, I am afraid. Reputation is everything, and with the business world being so accessible these days it is important to present a solid, dependable image to my clientele—some of whom have invested large sums of money—in my role as their fund manager. It is my professional responsibility to see their needs are met with efficiency at all times.'

'Who is your biggest client?' Ally asked, out of genuine interest.

'Paolo Lombardi,' he said. 'He has financial interests all over the world. Perhaps you have heard of him?'

Ally hoped her reaction to the name wasn't showing on her face. Not only had she heard of Paolo Lombardi, she had sat opposite him just a couple of days ago in Prague, discussing the mining portfolio she was responsible for in his company back home. What quirk of fate had brought this about? It had been the first time she had met Paolo in person, although they had exchanged many friendly e-mails and phone calls in the past. He was a lovely man in his early seventies who, as soon as he had sat with her over dinner, had drawn her out in a way few people had ever done. The thought of him blowing her cover was unthinkable— not yet, when so many questions were still unanswered.

She picked up her glass and took a reviving sip. 'The name is vaguely familiar…' she said lamely.

'He is about as big as you get when it comes to investment in Europe,' Vittorio said. 'I am not totally dependent on his goodwill, as I have many other important clients, the difference with Paolo is that he is Rocco's godfather. Believe me, it would not do to have him offside—especially right now, as the markets have been so unstable recently.'

Ally put down her glass with an unsteady hand. 'So you have to do whatever it takes to keep him happy, right?'

He smiled yet another of his enigmatic smiles. 'If it means marrying my brother-in-law's mistress, then I am prepared to do it for the sake of my business.'

She looked at him with wide, astonished eyes. 'You're surely not serious?'

He leaned back in his seat in an indolent pose. 'There are risks and there are risks,' he said. 'Unlike Rocco, I only make calculated ones.'

Fear beat like a tattoo in her chest as she locked her gaze with his. 'Are you saying you would go as far as making me your wife?' she gasped.

'I would only do so with certain conditions, of course.'

'Such as?'

'A prenuptial agreement, for one thing,' he said. 'I do not fancy giving half of my hard-earned fortune away if things do not turn out the way I anticipate.'

Ally was starting to feel more than a little bewildered. 'What exactly are you anticipating?'

He leaned his forearms on the table, so as to bring his face closer to hers. 'You would be an asset to me, Ally. You are beautiful and smart and young and healthy. We could make quite a match of things. I am at the time in life when I am thinking of settling down and producing an heir and a spare, as the saying goes. What do you say? Would you agree to be my wife for real?'

She jerked away from him in abject horror. *'Are you out of your mind?'*

He waggled a long finger at her reprovingly. 'You really should not bludgeon a man's ego so callously,' he said. 'I am offering you a lifetime of luxury. You will be generously provided for no matter what happens between us. I thought that was your prime motivation? Or do you change your mind as quickly as you change your hair?'

Ally stared at him in numb shock. She had totally forgotten

about her hair. It was such a stupid oversight on her part. Alex's hair was waist-length, and had been since she was a teenager, while Ally's had been shoulder-length for the last couple of years. Out of convenience she mostly scooped it up on her head with a clip, but tonight she had let it cascade around her shoulders, never for a moment realising the implications.

'I had it cut off recently,' she said, averting her gaze from his.

'It looks nice like that,' he said. 'It suits you.'

'Thank you…'

A silence descended like dust motes from the ceiling.

Ally took a deep breath and lifted her gaze to his. 'Vittorio…I think I should tell you—'

'The waiter is coming with our meals,' Vittorio said. 'Let us just pretend we are like any other couple enjoying a night out.'

'But I—'

'Ally, you are under no obligation to give me an answer until you meet the rest of my family,' he said. 'I think both my sisters will adore you. Chiara will be particularly relieved, now she does not have to worry about you posing a threat to her marriage.'

'Doesn't she realise what Rocco has done?' Ally asked in shock.

'No. That is the whole point of this exercise,' he said. 'I did not want her to find out about his involvement with another woman. That is why I want to take things to the next step. If we were to marry she would be totally convinced Rocco has not strayed.'

'But surely she has the right to know what has been going on behind her back?' she asked.

'My sister is vulnerable right now,' he said. 'She has been ordered by her doctor to have complete bed-rest. I do not want her to go into premature labour as a result of such a revelation. There is a tiny child to consider.'

Ally frowned as she looked at the food that had been set before her, wondering if her stomach would allow even one mouthful to go down and stay down.

'You are looking very pale,' Vittorio said. 'Is the food not to your liking?'

She picked up her fork and gave him a strained smile. 'No, it's lovely…really…it's just I'm a little stressed right now. I thought we were *pretending* to be involved. I didn't for a moment expect you would want to change the terms of our agreement. I'm not ready to take that step. I can't agree to such an outrageous scheme. It would be immoral.'

'We are attracted to each other, Ally,' he said. 'You have said you are no longer in love with my brother-in-law. Why should we not explore what chemistry exists between us?'

Ally could think of hundreds of reasons—one of them residing in a clinic only a short plane trip or train journey away. 'I'm not ready for a new relationship,' she said. 'Your brother-in-law hurt me. I don't want to risk such emotional trauma again.'

'I do not see how you could possibly be hurt by me,' he said. 'This is, after all, not a love transaction. I am being totally up-front with you over what I want. I want a wife and a mother for my children. I am prepared to pay for the privilege. All you have to do is sign on the dotted line and you will want for nothing ever again.'

She pushed her untouched food away. 'How can you be so…so cool and calculated about this?' she asked. 'You are talking about people's lives here. Not just yours and mine, but the lives of little children. Do you have any idea of what damage can be caused by ill-matched couples producing vulnerable offspring?'

'We are not ill-matched. Anything but,' he contradicted. 'The moment we met I felt something I have never felt before. I have the feeling you are the woman I have been waiting for all of my life.'

She gaped at him incredulously. Was he deliberately winding her up? How cruel could he be? Or was there some other motive? 'How can you say that, knowing what you know about me?' she asked.

His smile was tilted at a sexy angle as he leaned back in his chair and lifted his wine glass to his lips. 'What is it I know about you, Ally?' he mused idly. 'For one thing you were supposedly my brother-in-law's mistress, and yet I cannot help thinking you have never been in love with him. In fact I wonder if you have been in love with anyone. You have a look of innocence about you that is very endearing. In fact, if one did not know about your past, it would be all too easy to assume you were still a virgin.'

He was bang on there, Ally thought as she made an effort to pick at her meal, refusing to answer in case she implicated herself.

'The car thing troubles me, however,' he went on, watching her with that hawk-steady gaze of his.

Why did her sister do it? Ally wrinkled her brow every time she thought about it. 'I said I'd pay for it,' she mumbled as she tried to avoid his all-seeing eyes.

'And then there is the issue of the missing money,' he said with another cryptic smile. 'Do you still have it, or have you spent it all by now?'

Ally compressed her lips for a moment and then, lowering her gaze, mumbled, 'I have it…it's in my handbag. I was going to give it back to you… I was waiting for the right moment…'

'Keep it,' he said. 'The money is not important to me. The next few days, however, are crucial. If you act convincingly as my besotted fiancée I will wipe out all of your debts towards me. How is that for a bargain?'

Her head came up again, her eyes wide with hope. 'You really mean it?'

He smiled that killer smile again and, reaching across the table, gently brushed her chin with his bent knuckles. 'I mean it, *cara*. Now, eat up and let us paint the town together. Paris has a reputation for being the city for lovers, but Rome is just as romantic. I will show you what you have been missing.'

CHAPTER SIX

ALLY spent the next two weeks in a haze of late-summer heat. Although it made her skin slick with perspiration, it was nothing to the scorching heat of Vittorio's gaze every time it connected with hers. He showed her the sights of Rome, patiently explaining its chequered and at times brutal history, organising special VIP tours so she didn't have to wait in long queues with other tourists to see the many galleries and basilicas. The magnificence of the Sistine Chapel took her breath away, and in contrast the ruins of the Colosseum brought tears to her eyes as she listened to the audio guide Vittorio had bought for her.

He came up beside her as she looked over the arena and noticed the passage of tears rolling down her face. He frowned. 'What is wrong, Ally? Is the heat too much for you?'

He removed his cleanly laundered handkerchief and, instead of handing it to her, gently mopped the tears off her face, his eyes as dark as the espresso coffee they had drunk an hour ago, in a crowded and ridiculously over-priced café near the Spanish Steps.

'I'm sorry, but this seems to me such a sad place,' she said. 'It's like the *castello* we visited the other day, with its horrid torture chambers. How could people have done this to each other?'

He pocketed his handkerchief and took her by the hand. 'They are still doing it in various outposts of the world. Every day the news is full of such depravity,' he said gravely. 'Come, it is time for some retail therapy. My older sister is coming to meet you tomorrow evening. I want to get you a ring and a few other things that will assure her and her husband Sandro that this is for real.'

She stopped in her tracks and looked up at him. 'But it can never be for real, Vittorio,' she said, her eyes still glistening. 'You know it can't.'

His eyes darkened as they held hers. 'It is real for now, *cara*, which is all we have to concern ourselves with.'

Ally fell into step beside him, her arm linked through his just like any other couple in love. She could see hundreds of them around her. The happiness on their faces as they exchanged glances said it all, and yet it made her feel inexplicably sad. Would she ever find someone to love her the way she longed to be loved?

'Are you all right, Ally?' Vittorio asked as they walked some time later through the ruins of the Roman Forum on their way back to his *palazzo*. 'You are looking quite pensive all of a sudden.'

'Am I?' she asked, looking up at him. 'I'm sorry...I was thinking about...things...'

His dark eyes grew warm. 'What things were you thinking about?'

She drew in an uneven breath. 'I was thinking about what you asked me to do,' she said. 'You know...being your wife for real.'

His gaze dropped to her mouth. 'And what have you decided?' he asked.

She brushed the tip of her tongue over her dry lips. 'If I was someone else...someone who thought money was more important than love...I would seriously consider it. But...but I'm not.'

'So you are saying no to my proposal?' he asked, holding her gently by the shoulders.

Ally looked into his bottomless brown eyes and felt something shift inside her chest like a set of rusty gears. He was so damned irresistible when he looked at her like that! She had felt it every day for two weeks. She was going crazy in escalating anticipation of him taking things one step further. She could see it in his eyes, the way they kept going to her mouth, his own lips tilted in that musing way of his, as if he was just biding his time before he claimed his prize.

'Perhaps I have not demonstrated some of the fringe benefits clearly enough,' he said, moving closer.

Ally felt the brush of his strong thighs against her jelly-like ones. 'F-fringe benefits?' she croaked over a convulsive swallow.

He smiled and lowered his head, until his breath skated over the surface of her lips. 'Do you want me to describe them in intimate detail or should I just show you?' he asked.

When it came down to it, Ally knew she was hardly what anyone would call an expert on kisses, but as soon as Vittorio's mouth touched down on hers she knew she was being kissed by a master of sensuality. His lips were soft but strong, supple and yet demanding. The dart of his tongue was another thing entirely. Nothing could have possibly prepared her for its erotic insertion into the moist cavern of her mouth, the stroke and sweeping action making her feel as if every vertebra of her spine had been unhinged. She felt as if she was going to melt into a pool of longing at his feet.

Her own tongue was shy at first, tentative and cautious, in case she lost what little control she still had. But for some reason her natural coyness incited him to be all the more commanding. Her face was suddenly grasped by both of his hands as he deepened the kiss to almost blood-boiling point, his lower body grinding against the neediness of hers in a way that both terrified and tantalised her. She wanted more, but was frightened to ask for it. She didn't know how to communicate her need. How could she? She was a novice at seduction. She felt as if she was on a stage without a script, acting in a play written for someone else entirely. She didn't know what lines to say, what moves to make. All she could do was be herself.

But she wasn't herself.

The reminder was jarring enough for her to break the intimate contact. She pushed him away with both hands pressed against his broad chest, her breasts heaving as she struggled to regain control of her breathing. 'Vittorio, please…' Her gaze flicked anxiously to the amused crowd surrounding them. 'Everyone is watching us.'

'You worry far too much about what people think, Ally,' he said with a little smile. 'But then you are shy, *sì*? You are blushing like a virgin. You do that a lot, I have noticed.'

Ally felt a tide of hot colour pool in her cheeks. 'I'm just hot,' she said. 'I'm not as used to the heat as you.'

'What you need is a swim in my pool to cool off,' he said, and tucked her arm into his to lead her back to his *palazzo*. 'I will join you after I see to a few pressing business matters.'

Ally floated on her back in the deliciously cool waters of the plunge pool back at Vittorio's *palazzo*, relishing in the change of temperature against her skin. Ghita had left her a jug of chilled water with slices of lemon and bobbing chunks of ice, which had done much to restore her fluid balance and reduce the tight band that had been developing around her forehead.

Her mobile was next to her, and she had spoken to her sister's therapist, who had assured her Alex was becoming more lucid at times and that the new regime of medication was gradually evening out her moods. Ally desperately wanted to talk to her personally, but the clinic staff felt Alex needed a couple more days due to her high sedation levels before she had contact with anyone—even her sister.

The rippling of the pool water against her skin alerted her to the presence of someone else. Ally looked up from her prone position to find Vittorio within touching distance of her near-naked body. The water he had disturbed was brushing against her like a caress, and every movement she made to counteract it seemed to make it all the more intimate.

He surfaced just inches from her face, smiling that toe-curling smile of his, his long, dark sooty lashes dripping with water. 'You are like a mermaid, with your hair flowing out behind you,' he said. 'Are you feeling better?'

'Yes, much better. Ghita has been wonderful. I feel like a princess, being waited on hand and foot.'

'And so you should, as my fiancée.'

'Mistress,' she corrected him curtly.

'You do not think I am serious about this?' he asked.

'You are serious about diverting attention from your brother-in-law to you. So, *no*, I do not take any of this seriously.'

'So what would it take to make you take it seriously?' he

asked, moving so close she felt his strong thighs brush against hers underneath the water.

'Um…' Her mind went blank as one of his legs nudged between hers, touching her where her feminine form ached for him most. She could feel herself turning to liquid, could feel the instant melt of her bones, and she could feel her heart thumping rapidly—as if it would stop and leave her deadened and lifeless if he so much as moved away.

'We have kissed just the once, *cara*, and it set my blood alight,' he murmured against her lips, not quite touching but close enough to make them tingle with unbearable want. 'Why not see what else we can experience together, hmm?'

Ally was lost. She knew it, even though a part of her valiantly tried to fight against her all too ready capitulation. She was young, she was lonely, and she was unsatisfied and sick to death of always having to be strong and in control. There was something incredibly liberating in having someone else take charge for once. And Vittorio Vassallo was taking charge in a way she had only ever dreamed of. He wanted her and she wanted him. There was really nothing else that came into the equation. They were two people who had met under unusual circumstances and had instantly and very deeply desired each other. No one else had anything to do with what they wanted to experience, and yet…

Ally tried to shove the intrusive thoughts aside. This was about *her* life for once. Her twin sister Alex had made a mistake, but it didn't mean Ally had to sacrifice her own happiness indefinitely. For one thing Vittorio wasn't committed elsewhere. Yes, she still didn't know all the details of what had happened between Alex and Rocco, but she knew what had happened between her and Vittorio, and it was impossible to ignore. For once in her cautious life she was going to go with the flow, even though she was in very great danger of letting her heart lead her head— something she had never allowed before. But she didn't have the necessary road blocks in place to halt it.

He was like a fever, heating her blood to boiling point beneath the fine layers of her skin. Every time he came close she could feel every nerve in her body switch to high alert as the surface of her skin became desperate for the sensuous glide of his fingers or the simple brush of his lips, perhaps against her forehead, as he had made his practice if he thought someone was watching them, sometimes even when they were totally alone. Each tender action dismantled her defences; it was as if he was doing it deliberately, making her a slave to his sensuality—which indeed she was in very deep danger of becoming.

She could feel it now, his dark eyes roaming her barely covered form as they bobbed and bounced against each other in the cool water, their limbs intimately entwined. At one point she felt the hard bulge of his erection against her lower belly, and her stomach hollowed out in aching need.

Vittorio began to nibble with his tempting lips at the sensitive corner of her mouth, the stubble on his chin and his low velvet drawl unravelling every possible rational reason why she should push him away. 'Come upstairs to my room with me,' he said. 'I want you. *Now.*'

She kissed him back—tiny kisses, hesitant, shy kisses, that communicated her indecision as well as her growing desire. 'Should we be doing this?' she whispered against his mouth, her tongue flicking enticingly against his lips.

He placed a firm hand against the curve of her bottom and held her to his throbbing want, groaning deep in the back of his throat. 'How can you ask that, knowing what you do to me, what you have been doing to me from the moment I met you?'

'You've wanted me that long?' she asked, looking up at him in wonder, her heart beating like a trapped swallow in her chest.

He answered by lithely exiting the pool and offering her a hand to help her out. She locked gazes with his, her hand enveloped in the firm hold of his fingers, and knew there was no going back. She might live to regret it, but this was what she wanted—and she was tired of putting her needs on the back burner. For once she was going to feel like a woman and enjoy the pleasure of being worshipped as such. No matter what the consequences.

'I want you too…' she said softly, and followed him inside the cool shade of the *palazzo*.

CHAPTER SEVEN

WHAT followed next was beyond anything Ally had ever imagined could exist between two people. Vittorio was not in a hurry, which totally surprised her. She had expected a man with his sexual experience to zone in on his needs with perhaps just a cursory regard for hers, but if anything he held back to an almost torturous pace as her body blossomed and swelled under his expert touch, leaving her breathless and close to begging in his arms.

He uncovered what little there was to uncover, since she was still wearing her damp bikini, exploring each curve and indentation of her body as if it were a priceless work of art. After some exquisite minutes of this she became impatient to conduct her own exploration. She wanted to feel him, hot and hard and heavy in her hands. She wanted to taste him, to stroke her tongue over his length, to bring him to the point where he begged for the release she could feel building inside her like a volcano about to erupt after years of lying dormant.

She decided there was no point in shyness—not now, when they were lying on a coolly sheeted bed, the door locked and the film of sheer curtains fluttering at the windows, bringing in a late-afternoon jasmine-scented breeze that did little to reduce the heat of their writhing bodies as they moved together on the bed in an increasingly urgent mission to come together in the most intimate way possible.

When Vittorio's mouth began to suckle on each of her breasts in turn she felt her back arch, bringing her honeyed pelvis right where he could reach it with his taut erection.

'I do not want to rush you, *cara*,' he murmured against her tingling lips as he kissed her mouth again. 'You need time to prepare for me.'

'I'm ready for you,' she panted back, feeling the dew of desire between her legs.

He reached down and explored her intimately with his fingers, stroking, caressing, delving gently until she was crying out with the need for fulfilment. 'You are hot and warm for me, *cara*, but I must protect you,' he said, and reached across to search through his bedside drawer for a condom.

She watched in wide-eyed fascination as he applied it, his body so engorged and ready for hers she wondered if her small form would be able to stretch enough to accommodate him. Nerves fluttered like tiny moths in her belly as he resettled between her legs, one of his curled over one of hers to make his entry as smooth and deep as possible.

He took his time, nudging, retreating, thrusting a little deeper, until her slim form accepted his smooth thickness. She whimpered in delight. His body felt as if it was made for her. Every stroke and sensuous glide set off fizzing nerves of reaction right through her lower limbs, concentrating in the moist core of her, where every part of her seemed to be gathered in finely tuned focus for the final plunge into paradise.

'Relax and move with me, *cara*,' he coaxed. 'Do not hold back. Let yourself go.'

Ally was expecting some resistance, but apart from a tiny twinge at first there was none. He filled her to the hilt, moving slowly, tantalisingly at first, before he increased his pace. She was crying out at the sheer delight of feeling him inside her, the position he had adopted maximising her pleasure. She could feel it building, bit by bit; it was if she was ascending a steep precipice until finally the wondrous view was in sight. She hovered there for a moment, suspended in a world of wonder at all she had missed out on before. All she had to do was allow herself to finally tip over…

Vittorio heard her suddenly sucked-in breath, and then her breathless cries of release, and he felt something unlike he had ever felt before as she clutched at him in trusting submission. His body was bursting and burning to let go, but he wanted to savour this moment as long as he could. He had never had such a mind- and body-altering experience. In the past sex had been just sex. It was physical. He never allowed emotions to get involved. And yet this time…

She arched her slender spine and moved against him again, and his release began to pump out of him. He tried to hold back, but it was impossible with her body still convulsing in tight little aftershocks around him.

He lay on top of her, breathless, valiantly trying to garner some sense of the control he was so used to executing in situations like this. But he was at a loss.

He had not in his entire experience been told it could be like this. He had not understood how body and mind could be so inextricably linked, so that what she felt made him feel not so much a conqueror but an equal in every way possible.

And yet they were not equals, he reminded himself as he eased his weight off her slim form. He looked down and saw the slight stain of blood between her legs, where he had torn through what had appeared to be her innocence, and a blade of guilt assailed him. Although he had teased her about her shyness, he had not truly factored in the possibility that she was still a virgin. It made him feel as if he had exploited her in a way he had never intended.

He waited for her breathing to return to normal before he got off the bed and handed her a soft wad of tissues. 'Is there something you need to tell me, Ally?' he asked gently.

Ally scrambled to cover herself beneath the sheets. 'Such as what?' she asked, trying to sound casual and unaffected about what had just happened between them.

'You are bleeding. Is that your period, or something else you need to tell me? Did I hurt you?'

The question was delivered in such a tender and totally disarming way that Ally felt like confessing everything there and then. He was supposed to be a use-them-discard-them playboy, and yet he was concerned about the spot of blood that had stained his sheets and the possibility he had hurt her. It didn't quite fit her image of him as a ruthless playboy, but she didn't want to examine her feelings too closely again until she was alone.

'No…' she said softly, still keeping her eyes away from his penetrating ones. 'I'm having a period. I'm sorry…perhaps I should have told you.'

Vittorio narrowed his gaze as he studied her bent head and delicately flushed cheeks. 'My family is joining us for dinner later this evening. Will I send Ghita up to help you dress, or would you prefer to be alone?'

Ally forced her gaze to connect with his. 'I'll be fine,' she said, trying to affect a smile but falling a little short. 'I don't like to be fussed over. Ghita means well, but right now I would like to have some time alone if you don't mind.'

Vittorio lifted her chin, his thumb moving back and forth over the fullness of her bottom lip. 'You intrigue me, Ally. Call it male ego, if you like, but I cannot believe you are the same person my brother-in-law described. Either he is lying, or there is more to this situation than either of you are letting on.'

Ally moistened her lips. 'There is more to this, but…but I'm not sure what it is.' She swallowed painfully and continued, 'You see, I—'

His gaze intensified, making his pupils disappear into the blackness of his eyes. 'Yes?'

''Vittorio…there is something I need to tell you about Rocco and—' she swallowed '—me.'

'Let us talk later, when we will not be interrupted,' he said, as the noise of people arriving sounded from downstairs. 'My family is here.' He bent forward and kissed her forehead. 'I will leave you to prepare for dinner. Do not worry about my relatives. My older sister Justina is desperate for me to settle down, so you will be welcomed with open arms.'

'Is Rocco's wife Chiara going to be there?' Ally asked, trying to disguise her dread about meeting any of his family—much less the woman her sister had inadvertently betrayed by sleeping with her husband.

'No, she is under doctor's orders to stay put at our villa in Positano, but she is looking forward to meeting you as soon as she is well enough,' he said. 'Thankfully she is now assured that the rumours were nothing but a case of mistaken identity. She is convinced you and I are an item, and that Rocco is completely innocent.'

Mistaken identity, Ally thought on the back end of a sigh as the door closed behind Vittorio's exit.

Yeah, well, that was *exactly* her problem—wasn't it?

When Ally came downstairs she was a little disorientated, and found herself in one of the smaller reception rooms. It wasn't vacant, as she had first presumed, and before she could back out and find where the rest of the family had gathered she heard the clink of crystal, and saw a tall figure pouring a pre-dinner aperitif from a cabinet fitted into an antique wall unit. At first she thought it was Vittorio standing there, until the figure turned around and faced her.

She knew it was Rocco Montano, for even though his likeness to Vittorio was uncanny, considering they were not blood relatives, Rocco's lips were thinner, and right now were lifted in a snarl as he came towards her. The fumes of brandy on his breath wafted unpleasantly over her face the closer he got.

'What the hell do you think you are playing at?' he gritted out harshly. 'I told you never to contact me or my family again.'

Ally knew she would have to tread very carefully to get the information she needed. He was a man who had been intimately involved with her twin sister, and it would take all of what little acting ability she possessed to pull this off without him seeing through the part she was playing.

'How much more do you want from me?' he asked, with aggression carving every word to dagger points. 'I gave you what I could. What else do you want, you greedy little bitch?'

'What do you *think* I want from you?' she asked, watching every nuance of his expression as closely as she dared.

'For God's sake, Alex, you were supposed to go away,' he said, raking a hand through his thick black hair, his eyes shooting all over the place apart from anywhere near hers. 'That is what all the others have done in the past. Why not you?'

Ally planted a hand on her hip and gave him a gimlet stare. 'You should have told me the truth at the start. You owed me that at the very least.'

He let out an exasperated sigh and began to pace the room. 'I should have told you I was married when we met that night in London,' he said. 'I should also have told you I will never leave my wife. She is the reason Vittorio gave me a position in the company. Do you think I would walk away from that for a common tramp like you?'

Ally could barely stomach what she was hearing. People's lives—two young women's lives and happiness—had been bandied about like dollar chips on a poker table. It sickened her. It made her so angry she had trouble maintaining her disguise. 'So I was just a temporary fill-in? Someone to warm your bed while your devoted and trusting wife was back at home, loving and missing you?' she asked with caustic bite.

He sent his hand through his hair again. 'Did you do as I told you to do?' he asked.

Ally tried to read his expression, but it remained cold and distant. 'You should know me well enough by now to know I don't like being told what to do, Rocco,' she said, testing the water.

His eyes flared with anger, and something else Ally thought looked a little like panic. 'I told you to disappear,' he bit out. 'I gave you enough money to do so, for God's sake. What the hell are you doing here, in Vittorio's house?'

The door of the room opened behind them, and Vittorio's deep commanding voice cut the through the air like a knife. 'She is here because I want her to be here,' he said. 'And she will stay for as long as I want her to stay.'

Rocco swung around to face him. 'You cannot be serious!' he said. 'What has come over you? I told you she is mad. She keyed your brand-new car, for God's sake.'

'I am *not* mad,' Ally said, with steely emphasis.

Rocco turned back to Vittorio. '*Dio mio!* You were supposed to pay her off!' he ranted. 'Not sleep with her yourself!'

'I am at liberty to choose my own lovers,' Vittorio said. 'Unlike you, I am not yet married.'

Rocco threw his hands in the air in a frustrated gesture. 'What was I supposed to do?' he asked. 'Chiara was warned to take things easy during her pregnancy. Alex was more than available. She practically threw herself at me, like the slut she is.'

Ally snorted in disgust before she could stop herself. 'You low-life bastard!'

'So you chose a convenient lover to fill in for you, not for a moment thinking of the consequences?' Vittorio said, pointedly ignoring Ally's vehement outburst.

Rocco briefly met Ally's blistering gaze and hastily turned away. 'I thought Alex was a woman of the world. She told me she had been married and divorced. I figured she would be agreeable to a short-term affair. I did not for a moment think she would want anything long term. Nor did I expect her to toss in her job and follow me to Rome.'

Ally decided to remain silent. She didn't know enough about her sister's motivation to relocate to Italy. In fact she knew so little she was starting to think she had made the biggest error of judgement in her life. Exchanging places with her twin when they were ten years old as a mischievous prank was one thing; doing it when she was twenty-five was another thing entirely. This was certainly not child's play, and as each moment passed she felt she was sinking in even further over her head.

'It is of no importance now,' Vittorio was saying. 'The problem has been solved. Ally and I are intimately involved, and that is all the press and the rest of our family needs to know right now.'

Rocco sent Vittorio a penetrating look and switched to Italian. 'You *are* being straight with me, are you not, Vito? You do not have to pretend with me, remember? I asked you to solve this problem, not to take my place and sleep with her yourself.'

'But what did you ask *her* to do?' Vittorio asked with a searing look. 'Or should I take a wild guess?'

Rocco's eyes flicked to Ally and back again. 'She set me up, Vito,' he said in an undertone. 'The bitch tried to trap me. What else was I supposed to do?'

Vittorio had to fight hard to disguise his reaction. His gut clenched as if a powerful fist had grabbed at his intestines and cruelly squeezed. He felt his hands go to fists at his sides; although not a violent man by nature, he wanted to smash his brother-in-law's face against the nearest hard surface.

'You told me she stole that money from you,' he said, the pieces of the puzzle finally falling into place. 'But that is not what happened, is it, Rocco? You gave it to her, did you not? You gave it to her so she could—'

'Excuse me…' Ally inserted testily. 'But do you mind speaking in English when I am in the room? I find it rather disconcerting to be left out of the conversation, since I suppose the discussion has everything to do with me.'

Rocco curled his lip. 'You told him about the abortion, didn't you?' His cold gaze dipped to her flat stomach. 'I assume you had it performed, as I insisted? I gave you enough money— more than enough, if the truth be known.'

Ally felt her belly contract in fear. *Oh, dear God*, she thought in anguish. *Don't tell me this is what Alex has been through!* No wonder she had been so emotionally fragile, so close to the edge, as if nothing mattered any more—not even life itself. No wonder she had made such an unexpected attempt on her life.

'No…' Her voice came out on a strangled whisper. 'No…oh, please…no,' she said, the colour draining from her face. 'How could you have asked that of… of…?' She swayed and almost fell, her legs buckling beneath her.

Vittorio sprang to support her to the nearest chair, settling her into it and handing her a glass of water before he sent his brother-in-law a searing black glare that would have cut through a wall of diamonds. 'Do you have *any* idea of what you have done, Rocco?' he barked.

'I gave her the money to get rid of it,' Rocco said with no hint of remorse. 'I was going to pay it back to the company. How could I have a pregnant mistress while my wife was giving every indication she was about to lose our baby? It was the only thing I could do, but this money-hungry bitch refused to comply. She threatened to go to the press and tell them about our "love-child". I had to put a stop to it.'

Vittorio's expression was livid. 'So you told her to get rid of the child and get out of your life? How did you convince her to do it, Rocco? Or shall I make another calculated guess?'

Rocco wiped his brow again, his throat moving up and down as his eyes flicked in Ally's direction once again. 'I…' He paused. 'I told her if she did not have the abortion then she would find herself in danger of getting hurt. I did not for a moment mean to follow through on the threat, but I was getting desperate.'

Ally's head was still spinning. She could barely keep all her thoughts in some sort of order. They were like laser lights, randomly flashing off inside her head, making her feel sick to her stomach.

From the little she could string together, her sister had been coerced into having a termination. Ally knew her twin would have done anything to keep the man she loved—especially if she had been off her mood-stabilising medication. She wouldn't have stopped to think of the consequences, or at least not until it was far too late to turn back the clock. And once she had realised there was no future in her relationship with Rocco, the enormity of what she had been forced to do had probably caused her mental breakdown. It all made sickening sense. Her sister had hinted at the terrible guilt that plagued her, but Ally hadn't liked to delve too deeply until Alex was well enough to have a heart-to-heart with her face to face.

'You have been a complete fool, Rocco,' Vittorio said. 'For the last ten minutes you have not even noticed you have been vilifying the wrong person.'

Rocco frowned in confusion. 'What are you talking about?'

'Look at her,' Vittorio commanded. 'Look at her closely.'

Ally felt herself shrink into the French chair she was sitting on as both men turned their brown gazes on her stricken face.

'I do not know what you are talking about,' Rocco said, yet again wiping the beads of perspiration from his brow with his pocket handkerchief. 'I can assure you that is Alexandra Sharpe. You only have to look at her passport to confirm it.'

'That is exactly what I did do,' Vittorio said, in a voice that sent a lightning bolt of shock through Ally.

He knew!

She sat up straighter in the chair, her eyes like saucers.

When had he found out?

Her heart clenched as she thought of the intimacy they had shared such a short time ago.

Why hadn't he said anything?

She sat there, stunned. Perhaps not as stunned as Rocco, but certainly close. And she felt angry too. *Furiously* angry. Obviously Vittorio had been playing with her. For how long she didn't know, but just an hour ago he had slept with her, knowing she wasn't the person she had said she was.

Wasn't *that* taking things way too far?

'She...' Rocco swallowed convulsively as he stared at Ally, bug-eyed. 'She has a *double*?'

'A twin sister,' Vittorio informed him. 'Alex is currently recovering in a Swiss clinic from a suicide attempt no doubt brought on by your disgusting demands on her. As it happens, Justina's husband Sandro works with the doctor who treated her. Due to patient confidentiality there will be no leak to the press, so you can go home to Chiara before I feel tempted to do what I should have done a year ago and tell her what a two-faced creep you really are.'

Their conversation had slipped back into Italian; Ally couldn't understand much of it even if she had wanted to. She felt an overwhelming need to get out of the *palazzo* and as far away from Vittorio Vassallo as she could. All she needed was her passport and she would be gone.

Ironically, it was Rocco who gave her the opportunity, by suddenly launching at Vittorio in a tirade of angry abuse. Thankfully neither of them noticed her slipping silently from the room.

CHAPTER EIGHT

'How are you feeling?' Ally asked her sister, delighted in the change in her appearance. Gone was the gaunt, hollow-eyed look of before, and in its place was a freshness of complexion. Her deep blue eyes were now clear and full of hope, instead of dark and empty with despair. She had even put on a tiny bit of weight. Not much, but enough to fill out her cheekbones, giving her a healthier look overall.

'I am feeling much better,' Alex said. 'The counselling has been so helpful, and this new medication is making me feel much more normal. I will probably always feel bad about—' She choked up for a moment before going on, 'About the baby. But the counsellor has helped me accept it wasn't my fault I had a miscarriage. It was nothing I did or didn't do. The doctor told me one in four pregnancies ends in a miscarriage, but I don't think I really heard him at the time. I would never have gone through with the abortion, but when I lost my baby I lost all hope of getting Rocco back. And yet now I can't believe how dumb I was to imagine myself in love with someone so selfish.'

Ally's gaze went to the door of her sister's room, where a young man in a wheelchair was waiting patiently to spend time with Alex. Apparently they had struck up quite a relationship in the time Alex had been in the clinic. Andrew Claxton, a fellow Australian, had been injured in a road accident in which his best friend had died. Alex, in these last few days, had been one of his mainstays of support, putting her pain aside to help him cope with the slow climb back to reclaiming life.

It gave Ally much hope to see her sister concentrating on someone else's issues instead of her own. It seemed to signal to her that the emotionally healing process Alex so desperately needed was now well on its way.

And as for hers?

Ally was still struggling to come to terms with Vittorio's treatment of her. She felt used. She felt angry. And yet she knew a lot of the blame was her own. In her naïveté and inexperience she had stupidly fallen in love with him. And he had no doubt intended that to happen, in a twisted form of revenge for how she had deceived him.

Thinking back over their relationship, she found it hard to put an exact time on when he must have realised the truth. It made her cringe in embarrassment at the bare-faced lies she had told to his face. But some good had come out of it all, at least. According to the morning's newspaper, Chiara had delivered a healthy little boy, seven weeks premature, but doing very well. There was some comfort in that, if nothing else. At least Vittorio's mission had been accomplished.

He would soon forget all about his entanglement with her. In fact she wondered if he had spared a single thought for the woman who had spent just one magic, unforgettable moment— for her, at least—in his arms.

Ally gave herself a stern talking-to. He had spent many such magic moments with women much more experienced than she; he was probably congratulating himself that he had avoided a very public scene by her leaving without a fuss. He had made no effort to contact her, which suggested he had no intention of continuing their affair.

Alex was still holed up with Andrew an hour or so later when Ally next came to visit, so she retreated to the extensive gardens instead. Even though it was now close to the end of September, the leaves were only just turning to amber and red-gold hues. They fluttered to the ground at her feet in what seemed a half-hearted attempt to make way for autumn and then winter.

She heard the crunch of leaves under someone's feet and, expecting to see Alex's therapist, who often sought her out on her walks in the grounds, she was totally shocked to see the tall figure of Vittorio standing there.

'Hello, Alice,' he said.

She arched one brow at him. 'Don't you mean Ally?' she asked with a guarded look.

'You are one and the same, are you not?' he returned.

She turned away and kicked at some crunchy leaves with her foot. 'I can't imagine why you are here—other than to gloat over how you played me for a fool.'

'Is that not what I should be saying to you?' he countered.

She swung back round to look at him, her eyes blazing. 'You didn't have to sleep with me. That was taking things *too* far. I only did what I did to find out what had happened between Rocco and my sister. She wouldn't tell me all the details, and I couldn't find out any other way. I didn't expect you to seduce me. That was about as low as you could go, considering how… how I felt about you.'

'How *do* you feel about me?'

She glared at him. 'How do you *think* I feel about you?'

He waited a beat or two before asking, 'Do you love me?'

The question caught her totally off guard. She stood looking at him, her eyes as wide as dinner plates, her heart beating as heavily as a bass drum, her stomach tipping and tilting as she saw the glint of desire burning in his coal-black eyes.

'W-what sort of question is that?' she managed to croak, her heart still doing crazy back-flips in her chest.

'I need to know.'

'Why?'

'Because everything depends on it.'

'Your business, you mean?' she said with an embittered look. 'You do realise all I have to do is call Paolo Lombardi and tell him what a creep his godson is, don't you? Don't think I won't, because I tell you I'm sorely tempted to do so. And he would be appalled to hear of how you used me so despicably. I know I could convince him to remove his portfolio from your account. He has a lot of respect for me.'

'That will not be necessary,' Vittorio said. 'As soon as I realised you worked for the Australian branch of his company I spoke to him about my concerns over Rocco. I thought Paolo had the right to know what was going on, in case it somehow got out in the press. We had a long discussion, and as a result I have decided to terminate Rocco's position in my company.'

Ally frowned. 'But what about Chiara?' she asked. 'She's just had a baby. She'll be feeling so vulnerable right now.'

'Chiara is not as naïve as I thought,' Vittorio said. 'It seems she has regretted her marriage from day one, and once she has recovered from the birth she is going to ask for a divorce. It is the wake-up call Rocco needs. He will either turn his life around or continue along the destructive path he has chosen.'

'And what about what you did to me?' Ally asked with a frosty glare.

He blew out a sigh and shoved back his wayward fringe with his right hand. 'I am sorry I did not tell you I knew who you were when I initially found out. You left your handbag in the car that first day. When Beppe brought it in he dropped it in the foyer, and amongst the things that fell out was the money Rocco had insisted you had stolen. I was furiously angry, and was about to come back upstairs to have it out with you when I saw your passport on the floor at my feet. I picked it up, and of course one glance confirmed my suspicions.'

Ally wanted to be furious with him for allowing her to continue her charade while he had no doubt been laughing behind her back, but somehow she felt as if he had more to explain, so remained silent.

'From that point on I was concerned that Rocco was not giving me the complete story of his involvement with your sister,' he went on. 'I had no idea he had insisted she have a termination. Nor did I know about the threats he made towards her. I can hardly believe he would do such a thing. He was even prepared to see her face the authorities over the money he gave her. One assumes he hoped no one would believe her version of events. What he did was unforgivable. I cannot think about it without wanting to throttle him.'

Ally touched him on the arm, which stopped him in his tracks. 'She didn't have an abortion,' she said, looking up at his tortured and so beloved features. 'She lost the baby before she went through with his demand. She was off her medication. She has a condition… I don't want to go into the details now, but without regular medication she doesn't always act rationally. I think meeting your brother-in-law and what ensued was part of what led to a breakdown. She is on the mend now. She has even met someone who is clearly in love with her for who she is—which is what she needs right now more than anything.'

He cupped her cheek with the warmth of his palm. 'Is that not what everyone needs?' he asked, looking down at her adoringly. 'To be loved and accepted for who they really are?'

Ally's heart began to flutter about in her chest. 'I—I'm not sure what you're saying…'

He smiled and brushed the pad of his thumb across the cushion of her bottom lip, where the tip of her tongue had so recently passed. 'You could have ruined me. You had the chance in your hands and yet you did not do so. You said it yourself just now. All you had to do was talk to Paolo Lombardi and ask him to withdraw every single euro he has invested with me, and yet you did not. Why did you not take your revenge on me while you had the chance?'

Ally moistened her dry lips again, and raised her eyes to his. 'Because I don't believe in hurting the people I love,' she said. 'It's sort of my life's credo.'

'You love me, Alice Benton?' he asked, his eyes suddenly misting over. 'Enough to marry me as soon as it can be arranged?'

She blinked at him in surprised delight. 'You really mean it?'

'Am I not doing a good enough job of proposing, *tesore mio*?' he asked with a self-deprecating smile. 'Do I need to find some other way of convincing you I am for real?'

She gave him a pert little smile in return. 'Perhaps you could run by me those fringe benefits you mentioned a few days ago? I seem to remember they were pretty convincing at the time.'

His eyes danced with amusement. 'It will be my pleasure,' he said, and kissed her passionately and lingeringly until her head was spinning.

He lifted his mouth from hers after a few breathless minutes and asked, 'Now will you agree to marry me? Or do I have to kiss you again?'

Ally smiled as she hugged him tightly around the waist. 'Yes, I will certainly marry you. I love you, Vittorio Vassallo. I love, love, *love* you.'

He brought his mouth back down to the soft bow of hers. 'Then I think it is time you called me Vito,' he said, and sealed her mouth with a kiss that totally blew her mind.

* * * * *

ITALIAN BOSS, HOUSEKEEPER MISTRESS

Kate Hewitt

CHAPTER ONE

ZOE CLARK slipped the sunglasses off her nose to survey the discreet grey limousine idling at the kerb.

'Nice,' she murmured as the uniformed driver opened the door with a flourish. He'd already taken her one beaten up suitcase and stowed it in the boot.

Now she slipped into the cool leather interior of the luxury car and leaned her head back against the plush seat.

This was going to be a *fantastic* summer.

A smile bloomed and grew across her face as she leaned forward and flipped open the mini-fridge.

'Is this complimentary?' she called to the driver.

He stiffened before answering in heavily accented English, 'Of course.'

Zoe grinned and plucked a bottle of orange juice from the fridge. She'd rather have had the little bottle of cognac, but she didn't think it would be prudent to meet her future employer with brandy on her breath.

She took a swig of juice as the limousine pulled away from Milan's Malpensa Airport and into the teeming traffic.

The sky was cloudless and blue, the sun glinting brightly off the cars that zipped and zoomed their way across half a dozen motorway lanes.

Zoe sipped her drink, feeling the first familiar wave of fatigue crash over her. She hadn't slept much on the plane, and now a bit grimly she wondered if her employer would expect her to start work that morning.

For a moment she imagined him greeting her at the door of his villa, a feather duster and frilly apron in hand. What exactly did the temporary housekeeper of an Italian villa in the lakes do?

The job description had been surprisingly pithy—a scant two lines of tiny print in the back of the *New York Times*. Blink and you'd miss it. But Zoe had had a lifetime's experience of looking at such ads, circling them in red ink—usually with a pen that was sputtering or leaking or had lost its life altogether—before handing them hopefully to her mother.

What about this one?

There was always something better, something great right around the corner. There had to be.

The driver turned off the motorway, leaving behind the rolling hills of Lombardy as well as the endless traffic of the capital's outskirts for a smaller road lined with plane trees. Zoe glanced at the small road sign that read 'Como: 25 kilometres' before leaning her head once more against the soft leather seat and closing her eyes.

She must have dozed—she could sleep anywhere, except perhaps on planes—for when she woke the car was climbing higher into the hills, the dark green, densely forested peaks of the mountains providing a stunning backdrop.

She rapped on the dividing window, and with a long-suffering air the driver pressed a button so the glass slid smoothly away.

'Are we almost there?'

'*Sì, signorina.*'

Zoe sat back, taking in the ancient winding road, and the wrought-iron gates that presented themselves at intervals, guarding the wealthy residents within, whose villas could barely be glimpsed through the heavy foliage of rhododendrons and bougainvillea. As the car continued up the twisting road the lake shimmered enticingly at each bend, before disappearing again, and Zoe found herself turning around to look at it, to find its brilliant blue promise winking at her from between the trees.

'This is beautiful,' she said to the driver, before realising belatedly that he'd already pressed a button to return the dividing glass to its original place.

Then the car was turning smoothly into a narrow lane, and the driver spoke into an intercom affixed to an ancient crumbling wall. Zoe couldn't hear what was spoken, but after a moment the iron gates swung inwards, and the car proceeded up the lane.

Foliage crowded the car densely on both sides of the drive, so that when it finally fell away to reveal the villa Zoe let her breath out in a sharp, impressed exhalation.

Wow.

A sweep of jewel-green lawn led up to a villa that seemed more like a palace—a *palazzo*—than the villa Zoe had been imagining.

This place was a *castle*.

And she was supposed to clean it all?

She counted twenty-two multi-paned windows glinting in the sunlight before she stopped.

The car pulled round the circular drive to the front of the villa. A pair of solid oak doors, looking as if they'd survived the Dark Ages, remained ominously shut.

Zoe climbed out of the car before the driver could come round, earning his continued disapproval. He took her suitcase from the boot and deposited it on the crumbling portico.

'Here you are, *signorina*.'

It took Zoe a moment to realise he was leaving.

'Wait—you're going?' she demanded, hearing an annoying edge of panic creep into her voice. 'Don't you work here?'

'I am hired only,' the driver replied, his voice stiff with disdain, before he slammed the door and drove away.

As the sound of his motor faded into the distance, Zoe was conscious of how surprisingly silent it was. A bird twittered nearby, and the breeze, cool and fresh from the lake, rustled the leaves of the palm trees that fringed the great lawn.

The owner of the villa—her employer, Leandro Filametti—obviously knew she was here. Someone had answered the intercom and opened the gates. So why the silent treatment now?

Squaring her shoulders, Zoe marched up to the front door, lifted the heavy brass knocker and let it drop. A deep, melancholy boom reverberated through her bones—and hopefully through the house—and then there was silence.

Zoe waited. The bird twittered again, fretfully this time, its tranquillity disturbed. Zoe raised her hand to the knocker once more, her fingers curling around the sun-warmed metal, but before she could drop it to sound the boom again the door opened, pulling her with it.

'Argh!' With a surprised yelp she tried to disentangle her fingers from the knocker, and in the process nearly fell headlong into the man who had opened the door.

Firm hands curled around her shoulders and righted her once more. Zoe was conscious of a sudden sense of strength and power, although she couldn't really see the man in front of her. Once she was steady, she looked up, and found her breath coming out in a rush once more.

The man was beautiful. Zoe didn't know if he was her employer or a gardener, but she certainly liked looking at him. His hair was light brown and a bit ragged, touching the back of his collar. Eyes the same colour as the lake—a deep blue-green— were narrowed against the sunlight, or perhaps in disapproval. He didn't look very friendly.

Zoe straightened, unable to keep her gaze from wandering down the length of him. He was tall, a few inches over six feet, dressed in a faded grey tee shirt and worn jeans that hugged his long powerful legs. His feet were tanned and bare.

Zoe swallowed. 'Hello…um… *Ciao. Il mi…*' Her few words of Italian, snatched on the plane from a battered phrasebook, seemed to have leaked out of her brain. She smiled with bright determination. 'I'm Zoe Clark.'

'The housekeeper.' He spoke with little accent, his voice cutting and precise. He stepped back, opening the door wider, yet somehow the gesture still seemed unfriendly. 'Come in.'

Zoe stepped into a foyer, the black and white marble cool even through her flip-flops. The light was dim, and as her eyes adjusted she saw a sweeping spiral staircase in front of her, ornate and yet also clearly in disrepair. Her glance took in sheet-shrouded tables, and a bronze statue of a cupid that looked in need of some serious polish.

The man cleared his throat and her gaze snapped back to him. 'Are you Leandro Filametti?'

'Yes.'

The one word was spoken with a brusque flatness that made Zoe want to recoil. Instead, she jutted her chin and thrust out her hand. 'Nice to meet you.'

Leandro Filametti regarded her hand silently for a moment before he shook it. His touch was light, yet firm, and all too brief. He dropped her hand without ceremony and turned to walk out of the foyer, clearly expecting Zoe to follow—which, with some resentment, she did.

Leandro led her down a narrow passageway to the back of the *palazzo*. From the peeling paint and chipped woodwork, Zoe could tell the palace needed a good deal of TLC. More, she suspected, than her limited capabilities allowed.

Leandro stopped on the threshold of an enormous ancient kitchen. Zoe regarded the huge blackened range and the scarred oak table with both awe and dismay. A single plate and glass, she noticed, had been washed and placed on the drainer by the sink. In the huge space, clearly meant for cooking meals for twenty or more, they looked incongruous and lonely.

'You can start here,' Leandro informed her.

'Start…?' Zoe stared around. She couldn't even see so much as a broom—and, frankly, she wouldn't know where to begin. How did you scrub away years of grime and dust? Did you start with the cobwebs or the mouse nests?

'Yes,' Leandro replied, his tone sharp with impatience. 'You do know what housekeeping entails, don't you?'

'I do,' Zoe replied, her tone matching his. 'But I also know that my suitcase is still on your front steps, I've been travelling all night and I haven't even washed my face or had a drink of water.' Juice, perhaps, but not water.

Leandro did not even look abashed. 'If you'd like a few moments to freshen up, by all means take them,' he said, with just a trace of sarcasm.

'Could you show me my room?'

'Top floor. Take any room you like,' he replied. 'And you can get acquainted with the house as well as with your responsibilities.'

With that he turned on his heel and disappeared down another passageway, leaving Zoe open-mouthed and fuming.

She wasn't what he'd expected. Back in the sanctuary of his private study, Leandro ran his hands through his hair before dropping them with ill-concealed impatience. In truth, he hadn't known *what* to expect; he hadn't thought to expect anything at all. He hadn't considered the housekeeper he'd hired beyond her ignorance of Italian society and, most importantly, the Filametti family. He wanted someone anonymous; someone to whom *he* could be anonymous.

Yet when he'd surveyed Zoe Clark on his front steps, anonymous had not been the first word that came to mind. She was, in fact, all too familiar—all too similar to the women of his past. His father's past.

Fast and flighty. Cheap and easy. Unprincipled.

Even now his mind conjured the image of her standing there, dressed in a skinny-strapped top and shorts that showed far too great an expanse of smooth, tanned leg. Her hair, silky and dark, framed her face in choppy waves, and her eyes were a warm honeyed brown, almond-shaped and luxuriously fringed. Everything about her, Leandro thought, reeked of sensuality—a confident sexuality that he recognised, remembered. How he loathed that knowing feline smile, the glint in the eyes of a woman so arrogantly confident of her own paltry charms. And yet his father had fallen prey to those charms time and time again.

He would not be the same.

Yet even as that resolution fired his soul, another part of his body already recognised there was something about Zoe Clark that he both resented and wanted. She was sexy, and he was man enough to respond to it. That didn't mean he would act upon it. Ever. The world—*his* world—was waiting for him to make the same mistake his father had. To fall. To humiliate himself, his family, the ancient Filametti name. He knew it, had always known it, and even in the lonely solitude of the villa he recognised the dangers within himself.

He didn't need the complication of a sexy housekeeper; he didn't want it.

Except even as his fingers had wrapped around hers for that brief, tantalising moment, he had.

Leandro muttered an oath under his breath and sat down at the huge mahogany desk that had once belonged to his father. He hated that desk, its connotations and memories, yet some perverse part of his psyche insisted on using it. Redeeming it—or perhaps avenging it was the better term. He gazed sightlessly at the pages in front of him, with their endless equations, numbers and squiggles that represented a lifetime of research and achievement, and yet right now they signified nothing. He swore again.

The less he saw of Zoe Clark, the better, he decided. She could sweep and mop and dust and stay completely out of his way.

He didn't need distractions—and ill-timed, inappropriate desire was just one of many he'd have to push resolutely away.

Zoe found the servants' staircase—a steep, narrow, dismal set of steps—and cautiously made her way up. The gloom was intensified by a gossamer net of cobwebs suspended from the ceiling, and the only sound besides her own breathing was the resentful squeak of the steps as she made her way upwards.

She passed a dark, silent floor of closed doors and more shrouded furniture and then went up to the top floor, gazing in dismay at the four rooms available there. Each one was small and depressing, containing only a chest of drawers and a narrow bed whose mattress was questionable in both comfort and hygiene.

It was also stiflingly hot.

'At least the view is good,' she muttered, as she forced open a pair of peeling shutters and gazed out at the terraced gardens that ran down directly to the lake. The gardens were in as much disrepair as the villa, but they showed it less. Bougainvillea run rampant, Zoe decided, was pretty. Dust run rampant was not.

With a sigh she turned back to survey the room. Sweat trickled down her back and between her breasts, and with sudden clarity and determination Zoe decided she was not going to suffer up here while a dozen bedrooms below went unused.

Leandro Filametti be damned. She deserved a little comfort if he expected her to tackle this lot.

Twenty minutes later Zoe had settled on one of the more modest bedrooms on the second floor. Painted in a faded lemony yellow, it was a smaller room, whose shuttered windows afforded a stunning view of Lake Como. After locating a dented bucket and an old mop in one of the kitchen's many cupboards, Zoe spent most of the afternoon cleaning her own bedroom, airing the mattress and scrubbing and dusting what looked like a dozen years' worth of dust and dirt.

Why was this villa such a mess? she wondered more than once. It was a prime piece of property, yet it looked as if it had been empty for years.

She felt as dirty as the room had been by the time she'd finished cleaning, and she seriously doubted the villa was equipped with a decent shower.

The sun was starting its descent towards the lake, but the air was still sultry and warm. With a defiant shrug Zoe decided she'd make use of the natural resources on hand, and after slipping on a bikini she made her way downstairs.

All was silent, and Leandro was nowhere to be seen. Just as well, Zoe decided grimly. If she saw him, she might give him a piece of her mind—and that could get her fired.

She picked her way through the overgrown gardens to a set of stone steps that led directly to an old jetty. The water shimmered with late-afternoon sunlight and after a second's hesitation Zoe dived in, gasping as the shock of surprisingly cold water hit her near-naked body. She swam underwater for a few lengths, before surfacing and flipping onto her back, her eyes closed.

She floated pleasantly in an almost half-doze before she became conscious of another presence. She didn't know what alerted her, but something prickled along her skin entirely separate from the cool water. She lifted her head, treading water, as her eyes scanned the shoreline and came in direct contact with Leandro Filametti.

His expression was neutral, his eyes narrowed against the sun, his hands fisted on his hips. Even so, Zoe's heart slammed in her chest and she found herself strangely conscious of everything: her own rather bare body, the coolness of the water, the brilliance of the sun. And the cold, hard look she could now see in Leandro's eyes—could feel emanating from him just as if she were standing in front of a freezer.

He didn't speak, and Zoe forced a breezy laugh as she raised an arm in greeting. 'Come on in. The water's lovely.'

Wrong thing to say, she decided, as Leandro's neutral expression darkened into a scowl.

'I see you are availing yourself of the comforts of my home,' he said after a moment, and before she could stop herself Zoe gave a little laugh of disbelief.

'Comforts? I'm afraid, Signor Filametti, that your home affords very *few* comforts.'

In answer he arched one eyebrow, coldly sceptical. Zoe was getting tired of treading water, so she swam to the side of the jetty and hauled herself up. Sitting on the sun-warmed stone, dripping wet, she felt Leandro's gaze rove over her, and was conscious yet again of the skimpiness of her bikini. She was also aware that she didn't have a towel.

'What have you been doing this afternoon?' Leandro asked, his tone one that suggested Zoe had been lolling by the lakeside for hours, eating bonbons and reading novels.

'Making a bedroom habitable,' she replied sharply. 'When an ad says "room and board provided" it usually means just that. But none of the bedrooms in your villa were fit for human habitation, Signor Filametti, so I spent the afternoon making sure I had a place to sleep tonight.'

Leandro was silent for a long moment, and when Zoe glanced at him she saw his expression was as dark and foreboding as ever.

'I'm sorry,' he said finally, surprising her. 'I didn't think... I am involved in important research at the moment, and such considerations escaped my notice.'

Zoe jerked her head in a nod of acceptance. 'I couldn't find any sheets,' she added, a bit petulantly.

Leandro's mouth quirked upwards in an unexpected glimmering of a smile. 'Or towels, I suspect. Those I have, I brought with me. Although if I recall the beds on the top floor are single—'

'That shouldn't be a problem,' Zoe replied, 'because I chose a bedroom on the second floor.' She glared at him, ready for a battle, but after a tiny pause he just shrugged.

'As you wish. When you come up to the house I'll provide you with some sheets…' His disapproving glance took in her wet length once more before he added, 'And a towel.'

He shouldn't have gone down to the lake, Leandro knew. He was angry with himself that he had. He hadn't made the decision until he'd heard the sound of splashing and realised Zoe Clark must be down there. Swimming. In a swimming costume.

This realisation had presented his tired mind with far too many intriguing images that he'd pushed resolutely away. He'd been without a woman for too long—without companionship of any kind for too long. Normally a woman like Zoe Clark would disgust him. Bold, obvious, inappropriate, cheap. All the qualities he despised in a woman.

The few women he'd taken to his bed had been sophisticated, classy and most importantly discreet. They'd understood the nature of short-term, expedient affairs and they'd wanted the same thing. Pleasure. Satisfaction. And a painless goodbye.

Not, he thought grimly, money. Or, worse, love.

He didn't know what Zoe wanted, but he knew what women like her were capable of. And even if they weren't, he knew what the tabloids were capable of. He'd seen firsthand how whispers could destroy a person. Already he imagined the headlines if someone got hold of his situation: *Like father, like son. Leandro Filametti in a flagrant affair with his housekeeper.*

He pushed the thought—and the temptation—away.

Upstairs in the villa Leandro dug through the supplies he'd brought to the villa from his flat in Milan and found a set of clean sheets and a couple of towels. He should have considered the whole matter of her bedroom, but he hadn't wanted to consider her at all. Thinking about a housekeeper meant thinking about the villa, and even though he'd spent every day of the last month within its walls he didn't want to think about it.

He didn't want to remember.

As he headed downstairs his stomach gave a growl, reminding him that it was nearing suppertime and the only thing in the fridge was half a portion of pasta, left over from the restaurant where he'd eaten last night. He'd brought it home for lunch and forgotten about it completely. Somehow he didn't think Zoe Clark would consider it suitable fare—and she would be quick to point out that room and board meant feeding her too. He knew her type; she would insist on her rights.

The only option was to take her out to a restaurant. Of course there was always the danger of being recognised, but Lornetto was small enough and its few residents were close-mouthed and loyal. Annoyed, Leandro realised he was almost looking forward to the prospect of the evening ahead. He was being so weak…as his father had been weak. Grimacing, he headed for the kitchen.

He found Zoe dripping and shivering by the range, her arms wrapped around her sides. She dropped them as soon as she saw him.

'This kitchen is huge,' she remarked. 'I'm not sure where to begin.'

Leandro shrugged. 'You just need to clean it.' He thrust the sheets and towels into her arms. He couldn't keep himself from noticing the lithe perfection of her body, tanned and taut and so very bare. She wasn't curvaceous, but she had enough of a rounded shape to please a man and make his mid-section tighten uncomfortably. 'Once you're dressed, we'll go out to eat. Perhaps tomorrow you can go to the shops for food and whatever else you'll need. Do you cook?'

Zoe raised an eyebrow. 'That wasn't in the job description, but I can rustle up a few meals, if that's what you're asking. Is it just the two of us here?'

Although the question was basic, it seemed to reverberate through the air, conjuring up an uncomfortable intimacy, and Leandro instinctively sharpened his tone. 'Yes. I'll see you in a few minutes.' He turned on his heel, striding quickly out of the room before Zoe had a chance to say another word.

CHAPTER TWO

SHE shouldn't be looking forward to sharing a meal with as ornery a creature as Leandro Filametti, yet Zoe was honest enough to acknowledge that she was. She gazed briefly at her reflection in the tarnished mirror in her bedroom, happy enough with her appearance. No need to impress her employer, she decided, knowing that any attempt to do so would most likely achieve the opposite effect. She'd settled on a pair of jeans and a yellow silky top with skinny straps. She left her hair loose and damp, and eschewed any makeup. Leandro was waiting, probably counting the minutes or seconds to determine how tardy she was. He seemed the type.

Humming under her breath, Zoe headed downstairs. Just as she'd expected, Leandro was waiting in the foyer, and Zoe saw immediately that he'd changed. He wore a cream-coloured button-down shirt and tan trousers—a boring outfit if there ever was one. And yet on him it looked far too appealing. The sleeves were rolled up to expose strong, tanned forearms—how did someone closeted all day doing research get tanned?—and the trousers emphasised a trim waist and long, well-muscled legs.

Zoe tore her gaze away; there was no point ogling her employer. She didn't want to get involved with someone like Leandro Filametti, who could only see her as the hired help—a drudge to be treated with disdain or at best grudging respect. She knew how *that* scenario played out. But he was nice to look at.

'There is a restaurant in Lornetto, the nearby village,' Leandro told her. 'We can walk, if you like.'

'Sounds great,' Zoe replied breezily, causing a brief frown to pass over Leandro's face like a shadow. What a stickler, she thought, with a little burst of annoyed amusement. She wondered what kind of research he was doing. He was probably an accountant, or something equally dull.

Yet there was nothing dull about the flash of awareness that tingled up her arm when he took her elbow and guided her down the crumbling steps of the portico. He dropped it as soon as they'd navigated the wrecked stone, but Zoe was still conscious of a strange, shivery warmth where he'd touched her.

She shrugged the feeling away, determined not to be distracted. She hadn't come to Italy for a relationship; she'd come to get away from one, and she'd do well to remember that.

The sun set as they walked down the lane, leaving vivid violet streaks across the sky, and although the air was still warm and scented with lavender there was a hint of coolness too, as the evening breeze rolled in from the mountains.

They walked in companionable enough silence for a few moments along the lake road—La Ancina Strada, from Roman times, according to the guidebook Zoe had leafed through—until a village—no more than a huddle of stone buildings along a narrow cobblestoned street—came into view.

There was certainly something charming about the scattering of tables under a faded striped awning, Zoe reflected as Leandro guided her to an outdoor café along an even narrower side street. Dusk had fallen, and the night cloaked them in cool softness as he pulled out her chair. There was, she thought with an uneasy sort of pleasure, something almost romantic about the situation.

That notion was quickly dispelled as Leandro took a seat across from her, folded his hands in businesslike fashion and launched into an extensive list of her duties.

'I'm selling the villa,' he stated bluntly, 'as soon as it's in decent condition. You are required to keep it as neat and clean as possible. I understand the difficulty, since so much of it is in disrepair, but there will be workmen coming in to deal with much of the damage, and as their work continues so yours should become easier.'

Zoe nodded, although she hardly thought navigating work-men, falling plaster and all manner of unknown hazards would make her job easier.

A waiter came, and without a glance at her Leandro ordered for both of them. Annoyance prickled along her spine at this pre-sumption—although she recognised fairly that she knew an ap-pallingly little amount of Italian.

'What did you order?' she asked after the waiter had left. 'Just out of curiosity.'

'A local pasta dish,' Leandro replied with a shrug. 'Made with tomatoes and basil—simple enough.'

Zoe nodded. She wasn't about to kick up a fuss over some-thing so small, yet it still irritated her that Leandro had ordered for her without even asking. It spoke volumes about how he viewed his station in life…and hers.

And yet, she asked herself, determined to be honest, why should she care? She'd had years of experience in menial work; her impressive listing of chambermaid and waitressing jobs was undoubtedly what had secured her this position in the first place. Yet for some reason, in the enforced intimacy of their situation, it rankled.

'May I have a drink?' she asked a little pettishly, and Leandro's eyes narrowed, his lips thinning in obvious disapproval.

'The waiter will bring water—were you thinking of some-thing else?'

Zoe almost said she'd like a glass of wine after the day she'd had, but she decided she'd pressed enough. She shrugged her ac-ceptance instead and switched subjects. 'Why are you selling the villa? Is it a business investment?'

Leandro's expression hardened briefly and he shrugged in reply. 'Something like that.'

Zoe took a thoughtful sip from the water glass the waiter had placed on the table. 'Why is it in such a state?'

'Isn't it obvious? No one has lived in it for years.'

'Yes, but…' Zoe set down her glass. 'Why not? It's beauti-ful, and it's the type of property that would go in a heartbeat—or so I would have thought.'

'You know very much about real estate in the region?' Leandro asked with an arched eyebrow.

Zoe shrugged. 'I read gossip magazines. Celebrities are always buying up places like this for millions.'

'This villa hasn't been for sale.'

There was an ominously final note in Leandro's voice that made Zoe wonder what he wasn't saying. Still, she decided to drop the subject.

'You mentioned getting supplies in—would I find them here?'

'Probably not. Lornetto is no more than a fishing village. There is a market town across the lake—you can take the boat.'

'The boat?' The idea of jetting across the lake on her own gave Zoe an unspeakable thrill.

Leandro must have sensed it, for he narrowed his eyes. 'Have you ever driven a powerboat?' he asked. 'It is a small one, but still…'

Zoe opened her eyes wide. 'I'm sure I can manage.'

A reluctant smile quirked the corner of his mouth before disappearing completely, replaced by the more familiar disapproval. 'It is not so simple. I'll drive you tomorrow. After that…' He shrugged. 'We'll see.'

The waiter came to the table bearing two steaming bowls of pasta, fragrant with fresh basil and oregano. Zoe's mouth watered. She hadn't eaten anything all day, and she was starving.

Neither of them spoke as they dug into the pasta, and after a few moments Zoe became aware that Leandro was watching her with a mixture of amusement and disapproval.

'Do you always attack your meals with so much gusto?'

'When I haven't had anything to eat all day,' she replied, swallowing a mouthful of pasta, 'yes.'

Leandro did not look remotely abashed. Zoe wondered what kind of women he was used to. No doubt stick-thin models from Milan, who toyed with a lettuce leaf and called it a meal. Her mouth twisted in cynicism. He was wealthy, good-looking, powerful. Men like that liked ornaments on their arm, nothing more. Ornaments they quickly discarded…or shattered.

Pushing those memories away, Zoe smiled brightly at

Leandro as their pasta bowls were cleared. 'What kind of research do you do?'

'You wouldn't understand it,' Leandro replied, and her interest—and annoyance—were piqued.

'Try me.'

He shrugged. 'Risk analysis. I'm an actuary—I work in financial forecasting. Cashflow studies, you'd call it.' At Zoe's blank look he continued, amusement lurking in his eyes, 'Statistical modelling, stochastic stimulations, pricing role?'

Zoe shook her head. 'Nope, nope and nope.'

The amusement in his eyes made its way to his mouth, and Zoe's heart rate jumped and then kicked up a notch at the sight of his full-fledged grin. Did he know of its dazzling effect? she wondered, feeling almost dizzy. Was he aware of how it lightened his features, brightened his eyes, and made him all too approachable?

'I told you you wouldn't understand it,' he said with a shrug, and at this dismissal Zoe's heart rate settled right down again.

'Well, it's obviously made you rich,' she said bluntly.

Leandro's mouth tightened, his eyes flashing with something close to anger. 'Yes, it has. Although it is of no concern to you. I started my own company, and it has done well.'

Clearly he'd had enough of the subject—and of her—for he rose from the table, signalling for the bill with one autocratically raised hand. Zoe rose as well, and in a matter of seconds Leandro had dealt with the bill and was striding out of the restaurant, clearly expecting her to follow. He didn't look back, and with a little stirring of resentment, she made her way down the dusky street to join him, matching his brisk pace.

By the time they'd left the lights of Lornetto behind, the road was dark and filled with shadows. There were no street lights or passing cars, only the silvery glint of moonlight on the lake. Zoe stumbled on the uneven pavement and Leandro reached out to steady her, grabbing her elbow in a firm grip before she righted herself again.

'And you didn't even have a glass of wine,' he said, his voice a murmur in the dark. 'Although I think you wanted one.'

There went her heart rate again—skittering all over the place, stupid thing. Zoe could see his eyes and teeth gleaming in the darkness, but nothing more. 'How did you know?' she asked, a bit unevenly.

Leandro dropped his hand from her elbow, his face partially averted. When he spoke, his voice was coolly dismissive. 'A girl like you…what else would I expect?'

It took Zoe a moment to process his implication. She came to a stop in the middle of the road. 'What do you mean, a girl like me?' she asked, feeling a sudden icy pooling in her stomach. It was so close to what Steve had said, what he had *thought*.

Leandro turned around, exasperated. 'What do you think I mean?'

It was clearly a rhetorical question; there was no doubt, Zoe thought bitterly, in either of their minds what he meant. Resentment bubbled within her.

'The implication is hardly complimentary,' she said, her voice sharp.

Leandro just shrugged. 'It is what it is. Now, I don't fancy standing in the middle of the road in the dark. Let's go.' Without waiting for a response, he turned and started back down the shadowy road.

Fuming, Zoe followed.

A girl like her. If she felt like being charitable—or *he* did—she might think that simply meant someone who was fun, friendly, full of life. A few months ago she would have made that assumption—before she'd realised exactly what kind of assumptions men like Steve and apparently Leandro were making about her. *A girl like you.* Loose, easy, cheap. Basically, a slut.

Her mouth thinned and her eyes narrowed as she followed Leandro up the villa's private lane. The *palazzo* was no more than a huge shadow in the darkness.

She shouldn't be offended by Leandro's words, Zoe told herself. She shouldn't care what *a man like him* thought. She understood that going from place to place, job to job, made men think she was as loose as her lifestyle. And projecting a certain image—fun-loving, free—kept her safe. Protected her heart. She revelled in her reputation, in her freedom.

She could pick up or drop down at a moment, discarding homes and relationships with insouciant ease. That was who she was. That was who she *had* to be, to protect herself from getting hurt.

So why, for a moment, did she not like a man like Leandro assuming it?

A man like Leandro… What did that mean? She didn't know him at all, Zoe realised. He was rich, he was well connected, he was a buttoned-up accountant. No, an actuary. Whatever that was. But beyond the basics she had no idea what kind of man he was.

'The kind of man who thinks he knows all about a girl like me,' she muttered, and Leandro, now at the front door, turned round.

'Did you say something?'

'No.' Her voice came out in a petulant retort, but Leandro merely arched an eyebrow.

Zoe jabbed him in the chest with one forefinger; even with just the tip of her finger she could feel the hard definition of sculpted muscle underneath his shirt. 'You don't know me, *signor*. So don't go telling me what kind of girl I am.' She sounded ridiculous, Zoe realised distantly. She also realised her finger was still jabbed in his chest. And yet she didn't move it. If she wasn't so tired, if her brain didn't feel so fuzzy and light and disconnected, she wouldn't have mentioned anything. She certainly wouldn't have touched him.

Instead, her brain registered in that same disconnected way that he'd wrapped his own hand—warm, strong, dry—around her finger and raised it to his lips. His eyes were dark, and Zoe detected a spark of anger in their depths. She wondered who he was angry with. Himself or her.

She watched, fascinated, as her finger barely brushed the softness of his parted mouth. His eyes darkened even more, to almost black, and his mouth thinned into a contemptuous, knowing smile as he dropped her hand and it fell limply to her side.

'I wouldn't presume to tell you anything,' Leandro replied curtly. 'I don't need to. You say it plainly enough.'

With that he turned and disappeared into the darkness of the house, and Zoe realised it was the third time that day he'd walked away and left her standing alone.

* * *

He was playing with fire. Touching her. Needing to touch her. And enjoying it.

Leandro flung himself into his desk chair and closed his eyes, but he couldn't banish the image of Zoe Clark at dinner, wearing that silky top, her hair dark and soft around her face. He pictured the way her eyes had danced with amusement, the way those silly little straps had slipped off her tanned shoulders. The way he'd wanted to push them off.

And she would have let him.

He could still feel the barest brush of her finger against his lips— what had he been thinking, teasing her like that? Teasing himself?

He certainly wasn't going to act upon the latent desire that hummed inside him—between them. If he were a different man he might have. He might have said to hell with good intentions and higher principles, and taken what was so blatantly on offer. He'd enjoy it, for a time, and then he'd walk away—tabloids, colleagues, family be damned... All for the sake of desire.

But he wasn't a different man.

He wasn't his father, and he wouldn't cheapen and enslave himself to desire. Not for a woman like Zoe Clark—a woman like all the others who took and took and didn't care who she stepped on to get what she wanted.

Who she hurt.

It's obviously made you rich.

His mouth thinned in distaste at the memory of her words. Another woman on the prowl. Well, she wouldn't get anything from *him*. He wouldn't give her the chance.

Stifling a curse, he pulled his papers towards him, one hand fumbling for the spectacles he'd discarded on his desk. He switched on the desk lamp, and with a grim, determined focus bent his head to his work.

CHAPTER THREE

ZOE awoke to bright lemony sunshine pouring through the windows, a fresh breeze from the mountains ruffling the rather tattered curtains.

She lay still for a moment, enjoying the feel of the sun and the breeze, before memories of last night filtered through her consciousness and started to spoil her mood.

A girl like you.

You say it plainly enough.

Leandro Filametti had made it clear how little he thought of her. She shouldn't be surprised, Zoe knew. She'd faced far worse in her years as a chambermaid or short-order cook, in the endless parade of dead-end jobs she'd determinedly revelled in. Zoe Clark—the girl without a plan.

Tomorrow will take care of itself, sweetie. Hasn't it always?

And with the dead-end jobs had come the leering looks, the men who assumed *a girl like her* was always on offer.

And when she'd finally chosen to be involved with someone, to give her body and yet keep her heart safe, she'd still had her ego stamped on. She pictured Steve's sneering face before resolutely pushing the image away.

She wouldn't let Steve hurt her any more—she'd let him hurt her enough already—and she wouldn't let Leandro hurt her either.

Except last night Leandro's carelessly delivered condemnation *had* hurt. It had pierced her armour of indifference, and she didn't even understand why.

Why was Leandro Filametti different? Why did he make her feel different?

'He doesn't,' Zoe said aloud, her voice sounding strange, echoing in the empty room. She shrugged off her covers and jumped out of bed, determined to enjoy the beautiful day, so fresh and bright, and not to think about Leandro.

Not to care.

She was good at that; she always had been. And now would be no different.

The villa was silent as Zoe made her way downstairs, stepping through pools of sunshine. She skidded to a halt when she saw Leandro sitting at the huge kitchen table, drinking a cup of coffee.

'Sleeping Beauty finally awakes,' he said, his voice a mixture of amusement and acerbity.

'What—?' Zoe glanced inadvertently at the clock, and gasped when she saw what time it was. 'Eleven a.m.!'

'It must be the jet lag,' Leandro said laconically. 'In future I hope you intend to have a little *less* beauty sleep.' He rose from the table, taking his mug to the sink. 'If you're dressed, we might as well head to town. I can't spend all day fetching and carrying, and it's already near lunchtime.'

'Fine.' Zoe pushed her hair away from her face, and her stomach rumbled audibly.

A smile flickered across Leandro's features, then disappeared. 'And we'll get some breakfast as well.'

Zoe followed Leandro outside, through the gardens and down to the jetty, to where a weathered speedboat was moored. It was a small craft, clearly meant for functional use, yet despite its age Zoe could tell it was well made and expensive.

Like Leandro, she thought with a trace of humour. Nothing showy or ostentatious, nothing obvious, yet he still emanated the sort of arrogant assurance that could only come from a lifetime of money and power.

She repeated that mantra to herself as she climbed into the boat, sinking into one of the comfortable leather seats as Leandro slid into the driver's seat and the boat thrummed to life.

Zoe knew she should stay angry with Leandro, remind herself of all the assumptions he'd made, but with the sun sparkling on the water as if the lake were strewn with diamonds, and the day stretched out in front of them filled with enticing possibility and adventure, she found her indignation trickling away…at least for the moment. She slipped on her sunglasses as they pulled away from the jetty. The breeze was fresh, and just a little bit sharp.

'This is fabulous!' she shouted to Leandro over the sound of the motor. He glanced across at her, a smile lurking in his eyes, and suddenly Zoe wanted to see it on his mouth, see his face transformed, alive. 'Can you go any faster?'

For a moment his mouth tightened, as if he disapproved of the question, its implications and innuendoes. Then with a shrug he pushed the throttle forward and the speedboat jumped ahead, singing through the sea. A gurgle of laughter escaped from Zoe's throat, and she turned to see Leandro grin.

His teeth flashed white in his tanned face, his eyes, the same colour of the lake, sparkling with humour, and Zoe felt herself react, her heart skipping a beat, her insides tightening.

This was dangerous, she acknowledged, even as she grinned back. She knew what getting involved with a man like Leandro meant. What it felt like. Yet for that moment, recklessly, she *wanted* to be just a little bit dangerous. She'd keep her wayward heart under lock and key.

She held his gaze, silently challenging him, her grin changing into a seductive smile. He looked away first, his smile disappearing, and Zoe felt a flicker of disappointment. She sat back, enjoying the simple beauty of the alpine forests that stretched straight to the shore, dotted with the terracotta tile and crumbled stone of the region's many hamlets and villages.

After a quarter of an hour Leandro steered the boat towards the shoreline of one of the lake's larger towns. A promenade fronted the water, lined with villas, shops and street cafés. Leandro moored the boat at the public dock, and leaped gracefully out of the boat before extending a hand to Zoe.

She took it, not wanting to make a fool of herself by scrambling inelegantly out of the speedboat. And, she admitted silently, she liked the feel of his hand encasing hers—although he dropped it almost immediately.

'You should be able to get what you need in the shops here in Menaggio,' Leandro said as they walked towards the centre of town. 'Did you bring a list?'

She hadn't even thought of a list, but Zoe smiled brightly. 'Of course.'

Leandro's lips twitched even as his eyes narrowed. 'Why do I have trouble believing that?'

Zoe met his gaze directly. She was good at brazening it out; she'd had loads of practice evading landlords, bosses, men with groping hands and leering looks. Widen the eyes, smile confidently, keep the voice firm. It was easy. Too easy. 'I don't know. Why?'

Leandro shook his head. 'Because you don't seem like the kind of girl who even thinks about lists.'

Another judgement. 'You seem to have fitted me neatly into a box,' Zoe said, her voice a little shorter than she'd intended. 'And it's *woman*, please. Not girl. I'm twenty-eight.'

'Are you?' Leandro murmured, his tone and smile both sardonic. 'And don't you think you fit into that box?'

Zoe glanced at him sharply. 'No one belongs in a box. Not willingly, anyway.'

'Perhaps not,' Leandro agreed in a drawl. 'But even so the box can still fit.'

Zoe bristled, but Leandro ignored her, gesturing to a row of small quaint shops lining one of the town's squares.

'Perhaps we should have a coffee first, and you can actually *make* that list?'

'All right,' Zoe agreed, her voice still stiff. Hunger won over pride. 'I am starving.'

Leandro led her to a small street café, its tables shaded by brightly coloured umbrellas and situated perfectly to watch the lively bustle of the square.

Zoe's eyebrows rose when the owner of the café came out, speaking in rapid Italian, fawning over Leandro as if he were some kind of celebrity. Zoe saw a few other patrons glance their

way, heard the speculative murmur of hushed whispers and
wondered just what was going on.

Just who Leandro was.

Leandro answered the owner tersely before leading Zoe to a
table at the back. He ordered two espressos and a basket of
pastries, affecting an air of unconcern even though Zoe was conscious of a few more open stares and another round of whispers.

'You're famous,' she stated baldly, and Leandro shrugged, his
mouth tightening.

'My family is from this region, that is all.'

At least that was all he was going to say, Zoe realised,
although she imagined there was quite a bit more to the story.
Shrugging, she started to write her list on the back of a napkin.

After a moment Leandro peered over at her writing.
'"Cleaning supplies",' he read, his voice dry with amusement.
'That's a bit general, don't you think?'

'In *general*, I need everything,' Zoe replied. 'I looked around
yesterday and couldn't find so much as a sponge.'

'Fair enough.' Leandro shrugged. 'The villa's been vacant
for years, so I'm not surprised.'

'You mentioned it hasn't been for sale,' Zoe said. She'd added
'food' to the list. That was pretty general, too. All she'd seen in the
kitchen was a plastic takeaway container and a packet of coffee.

'Yes, I did.' Leandro's tone was guarded.

'Who owned it? And why did they sell now?'

The waiter came with the coffee and rolls, and Zoe took one
from the basket, biting into it with relish. Leandro watched her,
sipping his own coffee.

'They didn't sell,' he said at last, and then forestalled any of
the questions which had clamoured to Zoe's tongue by raising
one hand. 'Eat up,' he told her brusquely, dispelling any notion
of friendliness. 'We have a lot to do, and I want to get back to
the villa. You should, too. I'd like to see you earn your keep.'

The shops lining the square were small, yet surprisingly well
stocked. Within an hour Zoe had found nearly all the cleaning
supplies she needed, as well as the basic food provisions she
wanted to make some simple meals. Leandro arranged for it all

to be delivered to the boat, and they were heading back to the dock when Zoe saw a small outdoor market set up in another smaller, leafy square.

She skidded to a halt, strangely mesmerised. 'Oh, let's stop!' The stalls, with their barrels of spices and baskets of fresh fruit and vegetables, beckoned enticingly, unexpectedly. Kerchief-clad housewives haggled over bins of lettuce and joints of beef, their hard bargains tempered by shouts of laughter.

With a sigh and a little shrug, Leandro gave his acceptance, and soon Zoe was lost amid the stalls, touching fabrics, chatting in her broken, nearly useless Italian, happier than she'd been in a while.

When she'd said she could make meals, she'd meant it; but she'd envisaged plates of pasta with tinned sauce—staples from her nomadic existence. Yet now the ropes of garlic, the bunches of fresh basil, the huge rounds of mozzarella floating murkily in brine, made her want to be unaccountably domestic, providing real meals—meals for a home, a family.

Ridiculous.

She'd never had a family or a home—didn't even *want* one—and Leandro Filametti's decrepit villa hardly counted as one anyway. Still, she couldn't keep herself from loading up a wicker basket with plump red tomatoes and mozzarella wrapped in wax paper, a kilo of ripe peaches and the freshest asparagus she'd ever seen.

'I hope you're planning on actually cooking with this,' Leandro muttered, taking the basket from her.

Zoe gave him a quick grin. 'Absolutely.'

Half an hour later he finally pulled her away and they headed back to the boat. It was well after lunchtime, and Zoe had a brief spasm of guilt for having taken so long.

'I'll make you a really nice lunch,' she promised as they got in the boat.

'Never mind about that,' Leandro replied tartly. 'I'll settle for dinner. You can spend the afternoon doing what you're paid for.'

As soon as they returned to the villa, the bags and boxes were loaded into the kitchen, then Leandro disappeared into his study.

Zoe felt momentarily bereft without him; she'd enjoyed their outing more than she wanted to admit even to herself.

With a pragmatic shrug, she began to put all their purchases away. She'd start on the kitchen first, she decided. It needed a good scrub, and she didn't relish the idea of cooking in a such a dirty space. She wrapped a kerchief around her head, got out the new mop and sponge and set to work.

Three hours later the kitchen was as clean as it would get without a complete overhaul, and Zoe was filthy. She considered another dip in the lake, but decided to opt for a shower instead. She didn't want Leandro thinking she was slacking off the job… Except, Zoe asked herself in exasperation, why did she care what he thought?

Why did she care at all?

She never had before.

Even as she'd scrubbed and mopped he'd intruded on her thoughts. Questions, images, memories. Why had he bought this villa? Why had the people in the café recognised him and whispered about him? What was his life normally like? Did he have a girlfriend? A wife? A family?

Stupid questions, she told herself as she stripped off and stepped into the shower. Ones with answers she shouldn't care about, shouldn't even consider. She twisted the taps on and let the water stream hotly over her. Many of the villa's bathrooms looked as if their plumbing was at least fifty years old, but she'd found a renovated one on the upstairs hallway, and she revelled in the strong stinging spray.

Until the door opened.

To her credit, Zoe didn't even yelp. The shower door was fogged completely, so she could barely see Leandro…although she could make out that he was only in a towel, his chest bare and bronzed. She resisted the urge to wipe away the steam so she could see a little more.

And she wondered how much he could see.

Enough, she determined. For he froze in the doorway, and Zoe saw his eyes sweep her hidden length, felt tension and awareness stretch tautly between them, before, with a muttered apology— or was it an oath?—he slammed out of the bathroom.

Zoe leaned her forehead against the wet glass, her heart pounding, her head swimming. Even her knees felt weak.

Desire. Molten, liquid, hot. It coursed through her, stronger than she'd expected or even wanted. It made her wonder what Leandro was thinking. Feeling. And what might possibly happen between them.

Stop. Her mind screeched such musings to a halt. She didn't want to get involved with a man like Leandro. Hadn't she learned that lesson already? For a moment—a second—she pictured Steve's sneering face.

A girl like you... What did you expect?

A girl like you. The same words Leandro had used. The same condemnation. The judgement had hurt then, and she wasn't about to let herself feel that again. She refused to be used by a man who had too much power and wealth for anyone's good.

Even if he looked amazing in just a towel.

Still a little shaky, Zoe turned off the taps and stepped out of the shower, wrapping a thick towel around her, and another to cover her hair. Safely swaddled, she stepped out of the bathroom, glancing instinctively for Leandro, but he was gone.

And she felt disappointed.

Leandro raked his hands through his hair, his heart beating fast and erratically. He felt every latent instinct tightening into need at just seeing the vague outline of Zoe's delectable body.

From outside his bedroom he heard the bathroom door open and close, and cursed himself for hiding in here—away from her, away from temptation.

For he *was* so unbearably tempted. In that brief moment of seeing her fogged shape behind the shower glass he'd wanted her. He'd wanted to slide the door open and step under the spray, pulling Zoe's wet naked length against his, feeling her—feeling the smoothness of her skin against his palms, the sweetness of her lips against his. He'd wanted that touch, both the thrill and the comfort of a body close—joined—with his.

It would be so easy. The desire was there between them, stretching, simmering. Why not take advantage of it? Why not enjoy it and let Zoe enjoy it? He could be discreet; perhaps so could she?

Why not?

Such enticing, enchanting little whispers, stroking his conscience to sleep. He didn't use women. He didn't discard them as his father had, time and time again. He didn't let them enslave him, wrapping him around their little fingers, cheapening himself, his name, his family.

He wouldn't be that man.

It's not the same... You're in control. No one would know. There could be no scandal, no shame. Just mutual pleasure... Surely you can see that?

Leandro cursed aloud. Had his father had such thoughts? Been led astray by such damning whispers?

You've been without a woman for so long...what are you trying to prove?

Nothing. Everything.

Resolutely Leandro turned away from the door, away from the image of Zoe imprinted on his brain—away from the desire coursing through his body, convincing his mind just how easy— and wonderful—it could be.

Downstairs in the kitchen, Zoe pushed the memory of Leandro's intrusion into the bathroom firmly from her thoughts. It wasn't as easy as she would have liked.

She found herself becoming cross, banging pots and cupboard doors as she assembled the ingredients for a simple pasta dish.

She should just get Leandro Filametti out of her mind, she told herself. Maybe giving in to temptation would do the trick... For a moment she imagined it.

What would Leandro be like as a lover? How would he kiss? Would his lips be soft? She remembered the brief touch of them against her fingers and knew they would be. Soft lips for a hard man.

She exhaled loudly, forcing the treacherous images away. She wanted to be sensible. She was *going* to be sensible. She'd learned her lesson with Steve. She shook her head in self-disgust.

At least she'd *thought* she'd learned her lesson. Steve had been the first man she'd let close, and look what had happened. She might not have loved him—she wasn't *that* stupid—but she'd let herself care.

And she'd learned her lesson. Don't care. Not about anyone. Certainly not about a man like Leandro, who treated *girls like her* with careless contempt.

She turned her attention to the meal, determined to enjoy the simple pleasure of slicing ripe red tomatoes, the fragrant aroma of basil wafting through the kitchen. The sounds and scents of a home. While the sauce was simmering she went out to the garden and picked a bunch of soft pink oleanders, holding them to her nose to inhale their sweet fragrance.

She was overwhelmed for a moment by the simple pleasures of food and flowers. The large, dank space of the kitchen was somehow transformed by the bubbling pots on the stove, by the sense of space being used and enjoyed.

She was being silly, she knew, silly and romantic. But she couldn't help it. Somehow this decrepit old villa was growing on her, winding its way around her heart.

She didn't even notice Leandro come into the kitchen, and when he spoke from the doorway she gave a little jump, nearly dropping the flowers.

'That smells good.'

'Thank you.' Zoe busied herself with putting the flowers in an old glass jar.

'It looks much better in here too,' Leandro added.

Zoe dug a pair of ancient black scissors out of a drawer and snipped the ends off the flowers.

'That's my job.' She glanced at Leandro, her heart giving a now-customary lurch, and saw his hair was damp, brushed away from his forehead, curling along the nape of his neck. He was dressed simply in a white tee shirt and faded jeans that hugged his long muscular legs. Zoe swallowed and looked away. 'I thought we could eat on the terrace,' she said, turning to needlessly stir the sauce bubbling on the range top. 'It's so hot in here.'

'Fine.' Leandro was silent for a long moment, and Zoe kept her focus on the pans bubbling away on the stove. 'I'm sorry about earlier,' he finally said. 'I'll install a lock on the door.'

'Or just listen for the sound of running water?' Zoe returned, her voice somewhere between a scold and a joke.

Leandro was silent again, and Zoe almost looked around. Almost.

'I did,' he finally said, and she whirled around in surprise. He was gone.

By the time the meal was ready, the sun had set and the first stars were twinkling on the horizon. Zoe had laid the small wrought-iron table outside for two, conscious of the intimacy of the gesture. The soft night air swirled around her. The lights from a few boats glittered on the smooth surface of the lake, competing with the stars above.

Zoe gazed at the table and wondered if Leandro even expected her to join him. Perhaps he wanted to eat alone? In other circumstances she would never have presumed to share a meal with her employer. Unless he asked.

Why don't you join me? Steve again, reminding her of how pointless and pathetic getting involved with her employer was— how false this situation really was.

'Ready?' His voice, like a low hum, seemed to creep right into her bones and swirl around her soul. Zoe turned with a bright, fixed smile.

'Yes, I'll just bring it out.'

A few minutes later she came out onto the terrace with a large steaming bowl of pasta, returning to add salad, bread and a jug of water.

Leandro surveyed the spread with the barest flicker of a smile. 'I haven't eaten this well in weeks.'

'Takeaways and coffee aren't exactly a healthy diet,' Zoe agreed, and he glanced at her as she sat down.

'I imagine you survive on the same,' he said. 'Or similar. Am I right?'

Discomfited, she shrugged. It was no more than the truth, but she didn't want to be reminded of it now. 'I like cooking when I get the chance.'

'And when is that?' He'd placed a napkin on his lap and now began to serve them both pasta.

'When there's more than just me, I suppose.'

Leandro glanced up at her, his eyes heavy-lidded and sensuously speculative. 'And is there often more than just you?'

'You'd probably assume there was,' Zoe replied, a bit crossly. 'But, no, actually, there isn't.' She didn't let anyone get close enough. Or else she wasn't given the chance.

Leandro's smile widened briefly before he took a bite of pasta. 'This is delicious. Is it from a recipe?'

'I just made it up,' Zoe admitted, absurdly pleased by his casual compliment. 'I put in all the things I liked.'

'Why am I not surprised?'

She should be annoyed by his assumptions, Zoe supposed, but somehow she couldn't be. Not when the night air was as soft as silk, and the stars glittered like tiny diamonds strewn on a velvet cloth above them. Not when Leandro looked at her with that lazy sensuality that made her toes curl and her heart hammer and her mind go wonderfully blank.

And he was attracted to her, too. She could feel it—sense it the way you sensed a storm coming, when the atmosphere grew heavy and an energy snapped and buzzed through the air. She became achingly aware of everything: the cool heaviness of her fork—sterling silver, undoubtedly—the cool water sliding down her throat, the distant lap of the lake against the jetty.

Did Leandro feel it too? Was he wondering, as she was, what might happen after dinner? What *would*?

For suddenly there seemed a wonderful and frightening inevitability to their coming together. All her sensible self-warnings melted into nothing as the delicious tension stretched agonisingly, achingly between them.

They hardly spoke for the rest of the meal. Yet even so, as Zoe cleared the plates, she almost expected Leandro to come up behind her and wrap his arms around her waist. She was waiting for his touch, needing it, caution thrown to the winds, senses scattered.

But that didn't happen. He helped her carry the plates and bowls back into the kitchen, and then set about brewing coffee while she washed up. It was a strangely domestic and intimate scene, like that of a husband and wife. Or perhaps lovers. Zoe's whole body seemed to tingle with awareness and expectation as she waited for—what?

What did she want Leandro to do? What did she want to happen? Zoe pushed those questions out of her mind; now wasn't the time for thinking, it was for feeling. For waiting and wanting.

Yet as soon as the coffee was brewed Leandro took his mug and retreated to his study. Disappointment swamped her as he left, and the sudden heavy expectancy was dispelled, the storm clouds of desire blown clean away.

It was better this way, she told herself, struggling to be pragmatic. Better and safer.

It was late by the time Zoe finished with the dishes, and she prowled restlessly through the darkened rooms of the villa, taking in the swathed furniture, the paintings covered with sheets. The villa was completely furnished, she realised. Whoever had once lived here had left it suddenly, sorrowfully. Or was she letting her imagination run away with her?

Why had it been left to decay and rot? She felt like a magician, being asked to transform the empty rooms into something liveable and clean. A fairy godmother, longing to make the decrepit villa a happy place—a home.

Yet how on earth could she accomplish such a task? She, who had never known a home? Zoe gazed at the tattered drapes at the windows, suddenly remembering her childish effort at making curtains from a cut-up dress that had no longer fitted her. They'd been ridiculous raggedy things, the hems stapled because she'd never learned to sew. Yet Zoe had been so proud of them; they'd lent something warm and alive to the sterile hotel room with its plastic shades and stained bedspread. Her mother, however, hadn't even noticed.

Zoe sighed, the memory depressing her. Why was she thinking of such things now? Was it simply because she'd never cleaned a house—a home—before? She'd kept to hotels and restaurants, impersonal places, jobs and people you could walk away from.

And you'll walk away from this one…in three months.

The thought only made her sad.

She let her finger trace a line through the thick dust on a windowsill and realised again that she wanted to bring this villa back to life—which was stupid, since Leandro would just be selling it on anyway. And yet for the summer it could be more than just a property.

She stood by the window and watched the moonlight shimmer on the lake, imagined the people who had once lived here. Had they loved this home? Had they laughed and danced and loved in these rooms?

She wanted to believe they had. It was important to her, and she didn't even know why.

Isn't it obvious? a sly little voice mocked silently. *This is everything you never had.*

And never would. Leandro's voice echoed through her mind. *Girls like her* didn't have homes like this. Didn't want them or need them. She should never forget that.

A rustling from the drawing room's chimney startled her, and she jumped back. A trapped bird? Or a rat? Suppressing a shudder, Zoe backed out of the room, wanting to escape the alarming noise—as well as her own thoughts.

She decided to go for another swim.

Leandro was still locked in his study as Zoe came down in her swimming costume, a towel over her shoulders. She picked her way through the darkened garden, the scent of roses heavy on the sultry night air.

The stone of the jetty was cool under her bare feet and she surveyed the water gleaming blackly with only a tiny bit of apprehension before she dropped her towel and dived cleanly in.

She surfaced, the cold water a pleasant shock to her senses, and swam a few lengths before turning back. She was barely aware of a shadow on the jetty before someone else dived in, and a moment later Leandro surfaced a few feet away from her, his teeth gleaming in the darkness, his hair slicked back from his face.

'I thought I'd join you.'

Zoe's heart rate accelerated even as she tossed her head, pushing her hair back with her hands. 'How refreshing.'

'I thought so.'

The expectancy was back, Zoe thought hazily. The storm was coming. In a desperate effort to clear her head, she ducked underwater and swam away from Leandro.

What was she thinking? Doing? She knew what he wanted from her, what she wanted, and yet...

She wasn't ready to get involved again. To give her body again. She knew how little he expected from *a girl like her*. Was she willing to accept it? Was it enough?

Her lungs near to bursting, she swam to the surface—only to have Leandro grab her shoulder. She gasped aloud, and he turned her around in the water to face him.

'I thought you'd drowned!'

'I'm a good swimmer.' His hand didn't leave her shoulder, and a desperate, aching weakness flooded through her, making it hard even to tread water. 'I'm ready to get out,' she said, a bit stiffly.

Shrugging off his hand, she swam to the ladder by the side of the jetty. She felt Leandro's eyes on her as she climbed up, grabbing her towel and wrapping it securely around her. Desire and fear warred within her, and she didn't know which would win. Which she wanted to win.

Leandro hauled himself up, dripping wet and utterly magnificent. Zoe couldn't keep her gaze from roving over the taut muscles of his body gleaming in the moonlight. Her breath caught in her throat and her mind turned blank as sensation—the expectation of sensation—took over once more.

Leandro looked down and held her gaze, his eyes dark and compelling. Zoe forced herself to breathe. In. Out. And again. Despite her best intentions, her breath came out in a shudder, and Leandro lifted his hand.

Zoe stilled, tensed, waiting for his fingers to tangle in her damp hair and draw her inexorably closer. She wouldn't resist. Yet he didn't move his hand, and the moment stretched between them, suspended and endless.

Her head fell back, her lips parted. Her throat was open and vulnerable to his caress. Slowly Leandro let his fingers trail down her cheek, along her jaw, her throat working as he dropped his hand lower, to touch the vee between her breasts.

It was such a small, simple touch, and yet it left fire in its wake. Fire and yearning. Zoe swayed, and reached out a hand to steady herself. Her palm encountered the slick, taut muscle of Leandro's chest and she felt him jerk in response. She reached up with her other hand and laid it flat against him. They remained that way for a moment, suspended on the threshold, and then suddenly Leandro stepped away.

Zoe's hands dropped, her arms falling limply to her sides, and her eyes flew open. She saw Leandro's mouth harden into a thin line and distaste flickered in his eyes. Disappointment—and something deeper—swamped her.

'It's late,' he said brusquely. 'Goodnight.' And without another word or look, he turned and disappeared into the darkness.

CHAPTER FOUR

THE next morning Leandro was already enclosed in his study when Zoe awoke at the much more reasonable hour of seven o'clock. She dressed in her oldest clothes—a faded tee shirt and cut-off shorts—and after a cup of strong coffee in the kitchen determined to begin tackling the drawing room.

Faded yellow curtains covered every window, and when Zoe pushed them aside a cloud of musty dust rose in the still air. She coughed, wincing, and then moved to the next window.

Last night had been a wake-up call of sorts. Seeing the distaste in Leandro's eyes—perhaps it had even been disgust—had acted like a bucket of ice water, drenching her senses and her desire. For a moment or two she'd been wrapped up in the seductive promise of pleasure given and received. Shared. Of seeing her own desire reflected in his eyes, of feeling wanted. And perhaps she'd even deceived herself that it meant something more.

Well, it didn't. The look in his eyes had confirmed that. Yes, Leandro Filametti might *want* her, but that was all. And when the wanting was over he'd discard her, dump her like a bucket of dirty water, disgusting and forgotten. Like Steve had.

Zoe stilled, remembering the similar look of disgust in Steve's eyes. His snide rejection had stung her pride more than her heart, because she hadn't let her heart get involved—even when she'd finally given a man her body, she'd refused him her heart. Her love. Not that he'd wanted either.

Zoe's mouth twisted cynically as she plunged her mop into a

bucket of soapy water. She'd avoided love and commitment for so long she barely remembered what that craving felt like. That deep, endless well of need. And she didn't want to feel it again— the hope, the disappointment, the unfulfilled longing that swamped the senses and the heart.

Yet she didn't want a fling either. Her one attempt at a fling had left her more hurt and embittered than she ever wanted to be again. So what was left?

A sigh escaped her, a heavy sound. Nothing was left, and the thought was unbearably depressing.

She forced her mind away from such ruminations as she tackled the drawing room, mopping the old parquet floors with a determined ferociousness. She'd emptied the bucket of dirty water half a dozen times, and each time she'd hauled it to the kitchen she had found herself looking around for Leandro. She hadn't seen him at all.

Later in the morning a crew of workmen arrived to start on the roof, and Zoe glimpsed Leandro talking to them on the front driveway. He disappeared back into his study without so much as a word or glance in her direction.

At noon she ate some leftover pasta alone in the kitchen, half wondering if she should knock on Leandro's study door and offer him some. She decided against it, for her own sake.

After she'd eaten she offered coffee and some *biscotti* she'd bought at the market to the roofers. The three men threw up their hands and exclaimed over her kindness and beauty, with shouts of *'Magnifico!'* and *'Bella!'* as Zoe handed around mugs. She laughed, feeling cheered by their easy friendliness. *This* was the Italy she'd expected—not Leandro's taciturn disapproval.

'What were you doing?' He stood in the foyer, hands on trim hips, as she returned with empty mugs and a plate scattered with crumbs.

'Feeding the work crew,' she replied a bit tartly, even as her heart started skittering once again. 'It's hot out there.'

Leandro grunted his assent and Zoe dared to ask, 'Would *you* like a coffee? Biscotti?'

Leandro gazed at her for a long moment, his expression foreboding and yet also fathomless. What had she done to earn such disapproval? Zoe wondered. Gone for a swim? Acted a little light-heartedly? What made him—men like him, men like Steve—judge her so quickly and harshly?

Or was she judging herself?

'No,' he said at last, and Zoe almost thought she heard a thread of regret in his voice. 'No, thank you.'

He hesitated, and for a moment Zoe thought he might say something. Then he turned to go back to his study, and she went back to work.

By late afternoon the drawing room was resplendent in all its faded glory, the now clean floor and walls somehow emphasising the threadbare condition and peeling gilt of the antique sofas and chairs.

Zoe perched on the edge of a chair and surveyed the room with a strange aching pride. Afternoon sunshine streamed through the wide, now sparkling windows, pooling in golden puddles on the floor.

She'd pulled away the dust sheets from the furniture and paintings, intending to wash them—although she realised the villa might not even possess a washing machine. Yet even so she could imagine the curtains and sofas restored, the room blazingly beautiful once more.

With a little sigh she rose from the spindly chair and walked over to one of the paintings, an ancient-looking oil portrait of a rather austere man in nineteenth-century dress. Had he lived here? she wondered. He looked halfway to a scowl—so close to the way Leandro looked at her.

Then her gaze rested on the tarnished placard at the bottom of the picture, and her heart skipped a surprised beat.

Alfredo Filametti, 1817-1888. Her breath caught in her throat before she expelled it in a slow hiss. Glancing quickly up at the figure depicted in the painting, she realised there actually *was* a passing resemblance to Leandro—in the set of the mouth, the deep aquamarine of the eyes. Alfredo Filametti was Leandro's ancestor. The villa had to be his family home.

* * *

Her mind was still spinning with this new information as she showered, and then repaired to the kitchen to make dinner. She grilled some chicken breasts with lemon and basil in the huge oven, and tossed a quick salad. She set the meal on the terrace, looking forward to Leandro's company more than she knew she should.

At a little after seven, the meal she'd made steaming and fragrant, the table decorated with wild orchids from the garden, Zoe knocked on Leandro's study door—and was answered with an indistinct noise halfway between a snarl and a hello.

'Dinner's ready,' she called, and inwardly winced at how wifely she sounded.

'Leave a plate by the door,' Leandro barked back, and Zoe stiffened.

She shouldn't be hurt or disappointed, she reminded herself fiercely. Had she actually *expected* Leandro to eat with her every night? They might share a simmering attraction, but he was clearly showing her what kind of relationship he intended them to have now. And that was probably for the best.

She forced the feelings back, and even managed a shrug. 'Fine.' She took a plate from the terrace, unable to keep from noticing how romantic the table looked, with its flowers and fripperies. Unable to keep from feeling like a fool.

Resolutely she made him up a plate and brought it to the study, leaving it outside his door with a perfunctory knock. There was no response.

She ate alone in the kitchen, and afterwards took her cup of coffee out to the terrace, sipping it with a rather disconsolate air as she watched the sailing boats and pleasure yachts bob lazily along the lake.

Suddenly the summer stretched in front of her, endless and lonely. What was she supposed to do with herself all alone? she wondered. She could hardly expect Leandro to entertain her, yet she chafed at the idea of night after night spent alone, empty and aching with a need she could barely name… A need she'd always refused to acknowledge, or even feel…

She watched as a couple came out onto the prow of a yacht.

Even squinting, Zoe could barely make out their forms, although she suspected they were tall and slim and elegant. Rich. People like Leandro. Accustomed to wealth and power and luxury. People who looked down on skivvies like her.

She watched as the couple embraced, the woman's slim brown arms twining around the man's neck with sinuous ease.

They looked so happy, so in love. Zoe could almost hear the low murmur of their voices, the rumble of the man's laughter. They had everything, she thought with a sudden, surprising bitterness. Not just wealth and power, but happiness too. Love.

A pang of sorrowful longing pierced her, making her hurt in a way she'd kept herself from hurting for so long. Deep inside, in the empty well of her soul that insisted human beings were made for love, for togetherness and belonging, for a *home*.

She didn't want to feel this way. She'd come to Italy for an escape, not for a revelation about her life and its shortcomings. She *liked* her life; she always had. It suited her fine and it would continue to do so.

She'd never allowed herself another choice.

Zoe set her chin, forcing the sorrow and the emptiness—the longing—back deep inside, where it could stay good and buried. There was no reason why she couldn't enjoy herself this summer. Why she couldn't have fun. Lornetto might not be much of a hot spot, but there were surely other villages nearby, with bars, clubs—places she could go and meet people like herself. Girls like her, men like her, people who wanted to laugh and dance and have a good time. If you had a good enough time you forgot about the loneliness and the need. You filled up the emptiness…if only for a moment.

A little voice whispered inside her that she didn't want any of that right now—maybe not ever again—but Zoe pushed it away. She'd told herself she was going to have a fantastic summer, and she *was*.

'Where are you going?'

Zoe turned, her hand still on the handle of the front door.

'Out,' she said sweetly. 'It's nine o'clock at night. I assume my duties are over for the day?'

'Yes…' Leandro admitted reluctantly. 'But where do you think you're going dressed like that?'

Zoe glanced down at the strappy jewel-green sundress. It was on the skimpy side, but she hardly thought it deserved Leandro's look of contempt. 'Out,' she repeated, and added a smile that was only a little bit brittle with determination.

Leandro scowled. She hadn't even seen him in four days, and now he looked like a surly bear woken suddenly from his hibernation. He had several days' stubble on his jaw, and his hair was tousled, sticking up in a dozen different directions. He wore an old tee shirt and jeans, but the casual clothes just emphasised his lithe and yet powerful frame.

'Out where?' he demanded.

Zoe reined in her temper. She couldn't decide if Leandro had been avoiding her or was utterly indifferent to her presence in the villa, but after four days of non-stop cleaning and silent, solitary evenings, she was ready for a change.

'To Menaggio,' she said. She'd discovered a bus timetable in a drawer in the kitchen, and had realised she could get there on her own. 'Tomorrow's Sunday—my day off,' she reminded him. 'So don't worry if I'm back late.'

'What will you be doing in Menaggio at this hour?' Leandro asked, but the condemnation in his voice provided the answer.

'Having fun,' Zoe tossed back defiantly, and with a waggle of her fingers she flounced out of the villa, refusing to look back.

He had no right to interrogate her like that, she fumed as she strode down the villa's drive. No rights in her life at all. And she wouldn't think of him once this evening—she'd find a club in Menaggio, meet people, dance and chat, and have fun for as long as she liked. She *would*.

And she would like it.

Leandro stared unseeingly at the front door of the villa, the sound of its slamming echoing remorselessly through his mind. Zoe Clark had every right to do as she pleased in the evening, he knew.

There was no absolutely no reason why she shouldn't go out and enjoy the region's attractions. Yet the thought of her in some seedy bar in Menaggio, dancing and drinking and flirting, made Leandro's gut tighten and his mouth pull into a grimace.

Of course he should have expected no less. If *he* wasn't going to provide her amusement, she'd damn well find it somewhere else. He should be amazed that it had taken her so long. He knew what she was like—what women such as her were like.

Yet at that moment he wasn't thinking of his father's women; he was thinking only of Zoe.

He'd *liked* knowing she was in the villa—listening to her move about, sometimes humming or whistling under her breath. He'd caught glimpses of her wringing out a mop in the sink or washing windows, her hair caught up in a ponytail, and he'd felt that tug of desire.

He'd always retreated before she saw him, knowing he couldn't get any nearer. She was dangerous. *He* was.

He'd been avoiding her for days—ever since he'd come so close to pulling her into his arms after their evening swim. She'd been irresistible then, dripping wet, her skin almost silver in the moonlight. She'd wanted him, wouldn't have resisted, and that had made it all the harder to step away.

Even now he wondered why he had.

Why not take what was on offer? Why not enjoy it?

He could make his expectations clear; perhaps she wanted the same thing? A quick, easy affair. No strings, no promises.

He'd had such arrangements before—he was a man, after all—but they'd been with women of his own world, his own class, women he could trust.

Could he trust Zoe? He didn't know—and, worse, he didn't know if he could trust himself. Already he sensed in himself a deeper need for Zoe than he'd had for other women, and that was dangerous.

Suddenly he could hear his father's desperate, wheedling voice.

It never meant anything, Leandro... I couldn't help it... I was lonely... A man has needs...

And what of his family's needs? His family left bankrupt and shamed by his father's illicit lifestyle? What about his mother, left not just heartbroken but utterly destroyed by his father's faithlessness?

And was he, Leandro, going to act in the same manner? Chasing after whatever bit of skirt caught his fancy? Weren't the tabloids waiting for him to do so?

He wouldn't give them the pleasure. He wouldn't give *himself* the pleasure of sampling a woman like Zoe either. He knew what she was like—what women like her were capable of: selling their stories, blackmailing his family, holding out for more and more and more. Always more. Until there had been *nothing* left.

For a mere second he wondered if he was judging Zoe Clark too harshly. Yes, she was fun and easy, even loose—but a blackmailer? A thief? Utterly unscrupulous?

Leandro shrugged. Perhaps he was too harsh, but he refused to change his opinion. It was his safety net. The only thing that kept him from taking Zoe into his arms and making her his…to his shame.

He let out a growl of frustration and turned away from the door, heading outside to the terrace. The air was fragrant and cool, the evening light bathing the lake in shimmering golds and reds.

There were too many memories here, Leandro knew. They were haunting him, mocking him. Tormenting him. Making him feel—when he'd spent the last two decades refusing to feel, to care, letting his obsession be work, success. Wealth. Then there was no time to think—to remember all he'd loved and lost.

He didn't have to stay, he told himself. He could return to Milan, hire someone to oversee the workmen, the repairs. Zoe.

It would be running away.

He'd hidden from the past, from memories, for too long already. He knew this instinctively—had known when the villa had come into his possession that he needed to face its ghosts. And so he would.

He would face the ghosts of his past, of his family. His father. Exorcise and exonerate them. And then he would move on.

Yet meanwhile the days passed with painful slowness. He couldn't concentrate on his research—important research, that would bring him new clients, more money, even celebrity status in his profession.

What are you trying to prove?

He had so much to prove, to account for, that he ached with it. Burned with it. With the ferocious desire to atone for the past, to absolve his father's sins and his family's shame.

Having a fling with Zoe Clark would not help his cause at all. It would accomplish the opposite—taking him further from his goal, making him more like his father than he ever wanted to be. Yet, even so, he couldn't keep this other burning from consuming him, images and imaginings of Zoe leaping through his fevered brain.

It would be so easy…too easy. And too dangerous.

It was several hours past midnight when Zoe pushed open the front door to the villa with a cautious creak. Her feet ached both from dancing and walking; she'd missed the last bus from Menaggio and, after hitching a ride halfway, had been forced to walk alone in the darkness along the old rutted road.

It had not been a happy time.

To be truthful, the entire evening had been borderline wretched, a fact that annoyed her. She'd gone out in search of a good time, she'd been determined to have one, and she hadn't.

She'd moped instead.

Oh, she'd danced, chatted, flirted—done everything she could think of to ensure a successful evening. But inside she'd moped. Wanted to be back in the villa. Wondered what Leandro was doing.

Stupid Leandro, who probably hadn't thought of her at all. Why should he? She was just the slutty housekeeper.

'You're back.'

In the process of taking off her heels, Zoe froze, one hand still wrapped around her ankle. Slowly she straightened. In the gloom of the hallway she could barely make out Leandro's form, although his eyes blazed through the darkness.

'Yes,' she said inanely, and he grunted.

'I wondered if you'd be back this evening at all.'

Zoe stiffened at the implication. After a second's hesitation she threw back her head, smiling in the darkness. 'I didn't have *that* good a time.'

'No?' Leandro stepped closer, and with a lurch of something between alarm and attraction Zoe realised his chest was bare. He wore only a pair of loose drawstring pyjama bottoms. She could feel the heat radiating from him coiling inside her too. 'How good a time *did* you have, Zoe?'

She lifted her chin. 'Why do you care?'

Leandro was silent for a moment. Zoe could see the beat of his heart, the pulse in his throat, and felt her own jerk and leap in answer. 'I don't know,' he said finally. 'God knows, I shouldn't. Shouldn't even…'

His voice thickened, almost slurring, and Zoe held her breath as his hand reached out and brushed a strand of hair away from her face, his fingertips trailing her cheek.

'*Want…*'

Want. That was what was between them. Heavy and pulsing, a magnetic tidal force she had no strength or desire to avoid. She wanted it—wanted to be pulled under, to lose herself in the moment and the man… Even if that was all it was. A moment.

'Why shouldn't you?' Zoe whispered, afraid to break the moment for either Leandro or herself. Afraid to stop it, yet also afraid to begin.

'I don't know,' Leandro confessed raggedly, and then his hand stole around to the back of her head and he drew her unresistingly to him.

The first touch of his lips against her was sweet, tentative, tender as they tested and tasted one another. Yet even as that sweetness unfurled and bloomed within her it was already changing, deepening and darkening into something primal and ferocious and hard.

It took another split second to adjust, and then she felt the answering need blaze within her. She returned the kiss's ferocity, her hands coming around his bare shoulders, digging into skin, their bodies pressed against one another now, pressed and pushing, proving something.

Was she exorcising the memory of Steve and the shame he'd made her feel? Proving to herself that she could handle one more no-strings affair? Showing Leandro just what kind of girl she was?

But I'm not that kind of girl, and I don't think I ever really was.

Zoe pushed the questions and doubts away. She wouldn't—couldn't—think. Couldn't imagine what a man like Leandro had to prove—why he shouldn't *want*…want her.

For right now there was a great deal of wanting going on.

He pushed the straps of her dress off her shoulders, his lips hot and seeking on the sensitive skin of her nape. They both stumbled back and Leandro landed hard on the stairs—cold, slick marble against bare skin. Uncomfortable, difficult, and yet somehow it didn't matter, somehow it was still urgent and desperate and *angry*.

Why were they both so angry?

For that was the emotion pulsing to life between them, Zoe realised hazily as they exchanged kiss for kiss, brand for brand. It wasn't what she wanted, and from some inner reserve of strength she pulled away from Leandro, her bare back biting into the staircase's wrought-iron railing, and gasped, *'No.'*

Leandro was breathing hard, his face flushed, his eyes blazing blue fire. He dropped his head back, raking a hand through his hair.

'Cold feet?' he asked sardonically, yet Zoe heard the bite of another, darker emotion underneath his cynicism, and he didn't look at her.

'Something like that,' she admitted shakily. She pulled up the straps of her dress, covering herself. 'I don't want it to be like *that*,' she said quietly, after a tense silence when the only sound had been their ragged breathing as they recovered from the shock of experiencing something that Zoe didn't think either of them had expected. Or wanted. 'We're attracted to one another, obviously,' she continued, trying to regulate her breathing, her heart rate, her heart itself, 'but…not like that.'

Leandro half rolled away, his face and body averted from her, one arm thrown over his eyes. 'No,' he agreed in a low voice. 'Not like that.'

Zoe stared at him, at his dejected, defensive pose, heard the ache of self-loathing in his voice and wondered just what had happened…and why. She curled her fingers around the cold iron banister and hauled herself up.

'Well, then.' She'd meant to sound light, but there was a telltale wobble in her voice that made her wince.

Leandro didn't answer. Still sprawled on the stairs, his face averted, his head bowed, he simply waved one hand—whether in dismissal or entreaty, Zoe didn't know, but one thing was clear. He wanted her to go. So she did.

He *was* that man. Leandro listened to Zoe's heels click up the stairs and the distant slamming of her door before he let out a long, shaky breath. And then a curse.

What had he been thinking? Doing? Risking everything he'd worked for in a moment of lust?

He knew what he'd been *feeling*: desire, desperate and angry. More than he ever had before. He didn't *want* to want Zoe Clark. He didn't want the complications or reminders, the fears and suspicions confirmed. He didn't want to be pulled under by desire, to lose himself to lust when he never had before, when he'd always—*always*—been in control. A moment ago he hadn't been. A moment ago he'd wanted to lose control, to lose *himself*.

He wanted her too much, more than any other woman, and that was the problem. The danger. *He* was.

Leandro let out a shuddering breath. He didn't want to be proved wrong. Or right. He didn't know which it was, but one thing was glaringly, terribly obvious from this evening's encounter: he was his father's son.

Zoe walked to her room on shaky legs and aching feet. A slice of moonlight bisected the room, and in its silver wash she peeled off her dress, shrugged out of her underwear and fell onto the bed. She shouldn't feel this way, she told herself. She shouldn't feel so…*lacerated*. Her soul, her mind, her heart in tatters.

Steve had never hurt her this much, and the realisation that she'd allowed it only added to her pain. *Why* had she let Leandro affect her? When had she become so vulnerable?

She closed her eyes, longing for the oblivion of sleep. She certainly felt exhausted, yet sleep eluded her. Memories did not.

Leandro, his eyes darkening with desire, his fingers caressing her cheek, his voice confessing raggedly, *'I shouldn't want…'*

Why shouldn't he? Zoe wondered now, as she tracked the moon's voyage across the sky and waited helplessly for dawn. In her experience men like Leandro Filametti—rich, powerful, arrogant men, men like *Steve*—took what they wanted when they wanted, and damn the consequences.

Wasn't that what Steve had done with her? She still remembered the scalding sting of shame as he'd tossed a few crumpled twenties across the unmade bed. *For services rendered.* She'd thought they had a relationship; he'd seen her as no more than a prostitute—just another chambermaid in his daddy's hotel who gave a little extra on the side.

Zoe closed her eyes again, wishing she could block out that moment as easily as the moonlight. At least her heart hadn't been broken, because she hadn't given her heart to anybody. That had been her one saving grace.

Yet her pride, her self-esteem, her very *self* had been damaged in that moment. For Steve's careless actions had shone a glaring light on her life and its choices. Was this the kind of woman she wanted to be mistaken for? The kind of carefree, careless life she wanted to lead?

The life her mother had led?

She might have been far more inexperienced and innocent than men like Steve—or Leandro—assumed, but the fact that they even assumed at all hurt. She knew what image she projected, and she was beginning to understand its cost. It had kept her safe—yet had it really? Why was she now feeling so hurt?

She was on the brink of making the same mistake with Leandro Filametti that she'd made with Steve Rinault. And the frightening thing was this hurt *more*.

Except Leandro was no Steve. The thought made Zoe's eyes fly open, and she stared blankly at the moon once more. What was Leandro hiding? Why was he selling his family's villa? And why had there been so much anguish in his voice, his body, as he lay on the stairs and waved her away, a man broken by desire?

The questions swirled in Zoe's mind without answers, and as the first grey fingers of dawn edged the lake she finally fell into a restless, dreamless sleep.

She awoke to sun streaming through the window, filling the room with the heat of late morning. Guiltily Zoe threw off the covers and hurried to dress. She didn't need to be derelict in her duties on top of everything else.

Several workmen were hammering away on the roof as she came downstairs, making her wonder how she'd managed to sleep through the noise.

The rest of the house was silent and still, however, and a peek at Leandro's door showed it ominously closed. Forcing herself to shrug—not to care—Zoe got to work. Mop and pail, broom and dustpan.

She'd managed to clean most of the downstairs reception rooms, with their panelled walls and shrouded paintings—a few sneaking glances under dustsheets revealed more of Leandro's ancestors—and then she decided to head upstairs and tackle the bedrooms.

Cleaning was a mindless activity, and that, Zoe knew, was what she needed. Scrub and sweep and don't think. Don't remember the aching humiliation of Steve's dismissal, the fresher hurt of Leandro's anger. Or, even more painful, the endless well of loss and need of her unhappy childhood.

Can we stay here? Please, just this once? I like it here, Mum. I don't want to go...

Don't think.

Yet her thoughts kept intruding even as she washed windows and swept floors, feeling like a modern-day Cinderella without her prince. Memories, questions. Desires. Regrets.

It's better this way, sweetie. The next place will be better, I promise. Don't you want an adventure?

And of course she'd always blinked back the tears and smiled.

Yes, of course I do. Because that was the kind of girl she was— the kind of girl she'd made herself be.

Yet somehow, for some reason, being in this villa, being with Leandro, made her question everything she'd ever forced herself to believe.

Don't *think*.

'What are you doing?'

Zoe whirled around, a dirty dustsheet crumpled in one hand. Leandro stood in the doorway, dressed in faded jeans and a mint-green shirt open at the throat, looking fresh and cool. In contrast she was hot and sweaty, dirty and dishevelled, and at a distinct disadvantage.

'Doing my job,' she replied, a bit tartly. Already the sight of him was causing memories to stir within her; she couldn't quite take her gaze from the hollow of his throat where last night she'd put her lips and tasted the salt of his skin. And then asked him to stop.

'Yes, I realise that,' Leandro replied dryly. He wasn't smiling, but neither did he look as ferociously moody as he normally was. 'However, as you reminded me yesterday, today is your day off. Sunday.'

'Oh.' A blush swept over Zoe's face and she dropped the dust-sheet. When had she *ever* forgotten her day off? 'I must have…' Her throat was dry from the dust of the room. 'The workmen,' she justified lamely. 'They made me think… Why are they working on a Sunday?'

'I'm paying them extra to get the job done,' Leandro replied, a brusque note entering his voice. 'I need to get this villa on the market in the next few months. I hope they didn't disturb your beauty sleep?'

'No…' Zoe trailed off, wondering why she couldn't grin challengingly at Leandro and snap back a witty retort—something about how she didn't need any beauty sleep to begin with. That was what she would have normally done. Yet all her witty retorts and snappy rejoinders had trickled from her mind—and, even worse, from her heart. She didn't feel capable of making one, or even *wanting* to make one.

Instead questions clamoured in her throat, desperate for

answers. Why are you selling this villa? Why were you so angry last night? What is haunting you?

Who are you?

And who am I, wanting things I never did before?

'So.' Leandro cleared his throat, absently swiping at a few strands of cobwebs from the gilt doorframe. 'Do you have exciting plans for your day off?'

'No, I don't have any plans,' Zoe admitted. 'I suppose I could go for a swim…' Only that conjured up memories of her last swim with Leandro, the water beading on his moonlit skin, the kiss they'd almost shared, and she blushed again. What was *wrong* with her?

'In that case,' Leandro said, clearing his throat again, 'would you like to see some of the sights of the region?'

'With you?' Zoe blurted, the surprise in her voice cringingly blatant to both of them.

Leandro's mouth tightened, and his eyes shadowed before he managed a tiny smile. 'Yes, that was the idea.'

Zoe bent to retrieve the dustsheet, smoothing it out before folding it in an effort to hide her confusion. Why was Leandro asking her out? If that was indeed what he was doing? Was this a peace offering? Or an offer of something more?

What did he want? What did *she* want?

'All right.' She looked up, smiling, although Leandro's expression was carefully neutral. 'That would be nice.'

Nice. Such an innocent, innocuous word. Would this outing be the same? She didn't know, wouldn't think. She'd just enjoy, or at least try to. It was something—better than a day spent moping alone.

'Good.' He nodded briskly. 'I'll meet you downstairs in half an hour.'

'All right,' Zoe repeated, and then he was gone.

CHAPTER FIVE

ZOE showered and dressed quickly, choosing a demure pink tee shirt and khaki shorts, her hair swept up in a ponytail. It was armour, of a kind—a way to keep Leandro at a distance. She wasn't sure who needed the protection, him or herself. She refused to consider the issue too closely.

Leandro was waiting by the front door as she came down the stairs. He smiled briefly when he saw her, the cool smile of a friendly employer, nothing more, and Zoe knew they'd both put the boundaries in place, both donned the armour of an impersonal employer-employee relationship.

It was better this way, she told herself. Safer. So there was absolutely no reason to feel disappointed.

'I thought we'd take the boat,' Leandro said, and led her through the kitchen and the gardens to the shore.

A few minutes later they were seated on the speedboat, jetting smoothly through the lake's tranquil waters, the sun high and bright above.

'What are you going to show me?' Zoe called over the sound of the motor, and Leandro slotted her a quick, knowing smile.

'Everything.'

Zoe sat back and tried to ignore the tingle of anticipation—awareness—at his words. Had he meant to sound so provocative? Already the boundaries were slipping, changing. Weakening. And so was she. Because she didn't even mind.

She pushed her sunglasses down, determined to simply

enjoy the day and not second-guess everything Leandro
Filametti said. Not to wonder or want. It would, she knew, be
a difficult task.

Leandro glanced across at Zoe, reclining in the seat across
from him, her long, tanned legs stretched out in front of her.
She looked carelessly relaxed, yet he didn't think he'd been
imagining the guarded look in her eyes when he'd invited her
out for the day.

And why had he done that, precisely? He'd had no intention
of even seeing her today, having closeted himself in his study
before she'd woken. Yet he'd spent the morning gazing sightlessly at figures, listening for the sound of her steps on the
stairs, the slam of the front door as she went out in pursuit of a
day's pleasure.

By eleven o'clock he'd had enough, and had gone in search
of her. He'd looked on the jetty, in the gardens, expecting her to
be swimming or sunbathing or just lolling around. The last place
he'd expected her to be was upstairs, cleaning as if the devil was
driving her.

And his invitation had surprised him as much as it had her.
He couldn't fathom why he'd made it; he'd determined to ignore
her completely after last night. To forget her.

Yet he couldn't. And even now Leandro knew he was deceiv-
ing himself, thinking he could take his housekeeper to see the
sights as some sort of friendly gesture, something almost paternal
and innocent.

It was anything but.

He'd invited her out today because he wanted—needed—to see
her, to be with her, and the realisation ignited both his fury and
despair. Why must he be so weak when it came to this woman?
A woman who was totally unsuitable, ridiculously inappropriate.
A woman who reminded him of every showy, lipsticked tart his
father had picked up and paraded, to his family's shame.

And Leandro was just the same—taking her out, showing her
off… Didn't he realise how dangerous this was? How dangerous *he* was? At least when it came to Zoe.

* * *

They rode in silence for half an hour, before Leandro slowed and they approached a crumbling jetty surrounded by dense forest that led directly to the shore.

'An island,' Zoe said in surprise. A tiny island right in the middle of the lake, which looked practically deserted.

'Isola Comacina,' Leandro confirmed. 'Lake Como's only island. It doesn't have much on it any more, but it has a colourful history.' He tied up the boat, exchanging greetings with a wrinkled, round-cheeked man who sat in a rickety wooden chair on the jetty, presumably to welcome visitors to this undisturbed oasis. Zoe scrambled out of the boat, avoiding the impulse to take Leandro's extended hand, and he dropped it without a word.

'The island has been somewhat of a haven over the years,' Leandro told her as they followed a path from the shore to the island's heart.

The air smelled sweet and dry, and the forest cleared to reveal a meadow of long grass and a few twisted plane trees.

'Oh?' Zoe picked her way across the tufted mounds of grass, half wishing Leandro would offer his hand again. The chunky-heeled sandals she'd chosen to wear were far from practical, yet she was honest enough to admit she wanted to hold his hand for another reason. She wanted to feel its cool, dry strength, his fingers wrapping possessively—promisingly—around hers.

She wanted his touch.

'How is it a haven?' she asked, swallowing as she looked away from the sight of his arm swinging loosely at his side, his fingers within reach.

'The inhabitants of Lake Como—the wealthiest ones anyway—took refuge here when the barbarians swept in over a thousand years ago. The island looked a little different then—covered with houses and churches.' Leandro pointed downwards, and Zoe saw a foundation of ancient crumbled stone. 'Not much left now.'

'No,' she agreed. It was hard to imagine this lonely, deserted landscape busy and bustling with life. The only sound now was the rustle of grass as they walked through the meadow, and the distant cawing of a gull. 'What happened then?' she asked, and Leandro shrugged, his hands in his pockets.

'They had several hundred years of prosperity when they formed an alliance with Milan. Then Como and Milan declared war on each other, and soldiers came here and burned everything. A decree was made that nothing could be built on the island— no houses, churches or fortresses. That was over eight hundred years ago, and no one has really lived here since then.'

'I guess they took that decree kind of seriously?'

Leandro smiled faintly. 'I suppose. A curse was put on the island, actually, by Bishop Vidulf: "No longer shall bells ring, no stone shall be put on stone, nobody shall be host, under pain of unnatural death."'

'And that frightened people off good and proper?' Zoe returned, but a shadow had passed over Leandro's face, and there was a haunted, almost hunted look in his eyes.

'Yes… It must be terrible to live under a curse.' His words fell into the stillness, rippling and disturbing the tranquillity, and somehow Zoe felt he was speaking from experience.

'Well, here's one building that's still standing!' she said cheerfully, for they'd come upon a little church, with a high bell tower looking out over the little island.

'Yes, a few buildings remain. Fifty years ago this was a retreat for artists. Their cottages are on the other side, along with a hideously over-priced restaurant that caters to tourists.'

'Shall we eat there?' Zoe asked innocently, and couldn't help but smile at Leandro's firm shake of his head.

'Indeed not. There are far better places to eat.'

They didn't speak much as they wandered around the rest of the island, gazing at the ruins, with the lake sparkling like a jewel in the distance.

There was something lonely and sad about Isola Comacina, Zoe thought, although perhaps she was only being fanciful, thinking of the bishop's curse. Yet she wasn't being fanciful in noticing that a pall had come over Leandro's mood. He seemed guarded and distant, his mind on other matters, other memories.

What are they? Zoe wanted to ask, wanted to know. Yet she knew she had no right to such information. Still, she wondered what ghosts haunted Leandro, what had made him kiss her last night with such angry desperation before turning away in self-disgust.

They took the boat over to Bellagio, an ancient village with steep cobblestoned alleyways lined with flowerpots and sidewalk cafés.

Leandro led her to a café tucked away on a tiny alley. They were the only patrons, and the hostess, a smiling woman with greying, flyaway hair barely kept by a headscarf, fussed over them, bringing menus and bread and a plate of olives swimming in herbs and oil.

'Signor Filametti, è stato così lungo,' she exclaimed, and Zoe looked up with a jolt of surprise. She didn't understand the Italian, but she recognised Leandro's name. He was known here. He was known—just as he was in Menaggio.

He *was* famous.

And why shouldn't he be? Zoe reminded herself as she spread her napkin across her lap. If the villa belonged to Leandro's family—had done so for centuries—then of course he would be known in the region. Fussed over as a man of consequence, wealth, power.

Except he didn't wear his family's history and power like a mantle, with a sense of entitlement as Steve had. Leandro wore it like a yoke. A burden.

The realisation surprised Zoe, even though it was so glaringly obvious. After a few rather tersely exchanged words, Leandro opened his menu, effectively dismissing the friendly hostess, who promptly scurried to the back of the restaurant. Yet Zoe had the feeling that he acted more out of self-preservation than anything else.

'She knew you,' she commented, scanning the lines of incomprehensible Italian on her menu.

Leandro hesitated for half a second, his eyes on his own menu. 'Yes,' he replied flatly, and Zoe decided not to pursue that line of conversation.

'What do you recommend?' she asked instead. 'I can't understand a word.'

Leandro looked up, smiling faintly. 'I thought on your CV it said you knew Italian?'

Did it? Zoe bit her lip. 'I do—a bit,' she said. *'Sì, ciao, grazie…'*

Leandro's smile deepened. 'You're practically fluent.'

'I bought a book,' Zoe replied, her smile matching Leandro's. 'And I even looked at it once or twice.'

He shook his head, but Zoe could tell for once he was not annoyed. 'You're hopeless.'

'Why did you hire me, then?'

He glanced up, his expression sharpening. 'Because you suited my needs.'

'Which are?' She held her breath, waiting, wondering what he would say. Admit.

'Someone who doesn't know me or my family,' Leandro said flatly. 'A perfect stranger.'

His expression had darkened as he spoke, and when he turned back to his menu it felt like a dismissal. A rejection.

Yes, Zoe agreed silently, she was that indeed. A stranger. But why had Leandro wanted a stranger as an employee? It was an odd requirement, and one that made Zoe wonder yet again about his past. His secrets.

The mood remained sombre over lunch—huge plates of pasta and a shared salad that should have created a cosy, intimate mood, yet missed by a mile.

Leandro had retreated back into himself, and with a prickle of hurt annoyance Zoe realised she felt like an irritation to him now—as if she'd insisted on coming along rather than come by his own unexpected invitation.

'Where to now?' she asked as she followed Leandro out of the restaurant.

'Back to the boat, I should think.' Leandro scanned the sky. It was already well into the afternoon, and a few gauzy pink clouds streamed like ribbons across the horizon. 'I'll show you a tour of the lake's most spectacular sights from the boat, and then we should head back to the villa. I need to accomplish something today.'

'Important research?' Zoe surmised, falling into step beside him.

'Yes, actually. I have a client in Zurich, and my numbers analysis could affect the outcome of his bid by several million euros.'

'Wow.'

'Indeed.'

Back in the boat, Leandro perched at the helm, speeding them through the water with a distant, distracted air. Zoe gazed out at the gentle swells the boat created, trying to ignore the vague, yet growing sense of disappointment that gnawed at her insides and ate at her hopes.

What had she expected from today? From Leandro? Surely no more than what he was giving her—a friendly, if impersonal tour of Lake Como. Yet last night and all of its implications remained between them, unspoken, stretching the silence as taut as a wire. For a moment Zoe relived the touch of Leandro's lips on hers, his hands on her body, skin against skin.

Had it really been no more than a mistake? An aberration? It seemed that was how Leandro was going to view it. And there had been something *wrong* about it—something angry. Yet even that realisation could not keep her from remembering the sweetness of his touch, and Zoe sighed, restless, unsatisfied, not knowing what she wanted or how she could even begin to get it. If Leandro could even provide it… For surely she wanted more than he was willing to give?

Leandro cut the motor, and they were both plunged into a tranquil silence that somehow made Zoe feel more tense than ever. He pointed at the near shore.

'Villa Carlotta.'

Zoe glanced at the villa whose impressive façade was reflected in the still water. The densely forested mountain towered behind, the tops of the trees reaching for a few wispy clouds. The terraced gardens, surrounded by hedges, led right down to the water. It was like looking at a postcard—something too fabulous to be real.

'It's amazing,' she said, and Leandro nodded.

'One of the more spectacular villas on the lake.'

'Yours is pretty spectacular,' Zoe ventured, trying for a light tone. Leandro just shrugged. 'It *is* yours, isn't it?' she pressed.

She didn't look at him, but leaned over the side of the boat to trail her fingers through the smooth silky water.

'Of course it is,' Leandro replied.

'I mean it belongs to your family.' Her words seemed to fall into the silence, rippling and disturbing the stillness just as her fingers were. 'I saw some paintings as I was cleaning. Portraits of your ancestors. Filamettis.'

'Ah.' Leandro's fingers clenched around the steering wheel, his knuckles whitening, although his tone was deceptively light. *Still*, Zoe wasn't fooled. 'Well, yes, as a matter of fact. It has been in the Filametti family for generations. But it now belongs to me.' There was implacable resolution, a hardness to his tone, and he turned his head away from her, squinting into the sunlight.

'But why are you selling it?' Zoe blurted. 'It's your family's. It must have such a history, a *legacy*—'

'That it does.' Leandro shrugged one shoulder, his muscles rippling under his shirt. 'But it's not one I admire or care for, so it hardly matters.'

That, Zoe thought, was not true. Oh, she believed the first part, but not the second. Every line of Leandro's powerful body was taut with tension, with suppressed anger. Whatever his family's legacy was, it mattered very much indeed.

'Did you ever live there before?' she asked, and Leandro was silent for so long Zoe didn't think he was going to answer.

'Yes,' he finally said tightly.

'For how long?'

'Thirteen years, as you're so curious. I grew up there.'

Zoe shook her head slowly. She thought of the rooms full of antiques, portraits and keepsakes of a family that stretched on for generations. She remembered her fanciful imaginings of the people who'd lived and loved there. Leandro had, his ancestors had, for hundreds of years.

It was a dizzying thought for someone like her—someone who had no family or home, who knew no one but the mother who refused to answer questions, who preferred to pretend they'd both somehow sprung fully formed upon this earth, like Venus from the waves.

So much history, so much heritage, so many people and memories. And Leandro was giving it all away as if it was worth nothing. 'I can't believe you're selling it,' she said, her voice somewhere between a sigh and a scold, and Leandro turned to look at her sharply.

'Why shouldn't I? I can hardly live there now.'

'Why not? Or at least when you marry, start a family—' She swallowed, her mind suddenly filled with images of Leandro playing happy families—a child on his shoulder, an elegant, *appropriate* wife by his side.

'I'm not going to marry or start a family,' Leandro stated flatly.

Zoe raised her eyebrows. 'Ever?'

'Ever,' he confirmed with a cold smile. 'I shouldn't think that would surprise *you*,' he continued. 'You don't seem the marrying kind either.'

'Don't I?' Zoe kept her voice light, but she bent her head, letting her hair fall forward as she trailed her fingers through the cool water again. She didn't want Leandro to see how much those words stung. Hurt.

'No, you don't,' he told her, his voice blunt and hard.

Zoe stiffened and looked up, and saw him gazing at her with a critical shrewdness that she didn't like. At all.

'You seem like the kind of girl who takes what she can get when she can get it. Who enjoys the ride and damns the consequences. Who doesn't care…about anything.'

His voice was cutting, brutal, and Zoe blinked under the verbal onslaught. She was too shocked to feel anything at first, but as Leandro flicked the motor back on the feelings came. Hurt and humiliation, causing her cheeks to flush and her eyes to sting, making her remember the money Steve had thrown across the bed as he'd sneeringly told her he'd had enough.

Yet this wasn't about Steve. It was about Leandro—the man sitting across from her, his body taut with tension and memory, his words an accusation and a judgement.

Anger fired through her, fuelling her. She reached out and grabbed Leandro's arm, forcing him to slow the boat. He turned his head, his eyes flashing, his mouth no more than a thin, hard line.

'You don't know anything about me,' Zoe said, her voice clear and hard.

Leandro's lips thinned into a cold smile. 'I've seen and experienced enough.'

'Oh?' She raised one eyebrow, still high on outrage. 'You want to make assumptions, Leandro? Then I'll go ahead and make a few of my own. You're a man who is completely blinded by his past. I don't know what your family did or didn't do that's made you so disgusted, so angry, but I do know that if I had a house like that—a *history* like that—I wouldn't go throwing it away. I wouldn't spit on it the way you are.'

'You don't know—'

'No, I don't. And you don't know me either. You have no idea who I am or where I come from, what I've lived or seen or felt. *You don't know.*' Her voice shook, and she felt tears at the corners of her eyes. She drew a shaky breath and forced herself to continue. 'So why don't you just keep your lousy assumptions to yourself and take me home? Or should I just say back to the villa, since it obviously was never a home to you?'

Leandro stared at her for a long moment, his face expressionless, ominously blank. Then with a jerky nod he pushed hard on the throttle, sending them skimming across the water in angry silence.

They didn't speak as Leandro tied the boat up to the dock, and Zoe scrambled onto the jetty without his help. Once inside the villa he disappeared into his study, and Zoe made her way upstairs to the sanctuary of her bedroom.

Except no respite was to be found there. She lay on the bed and watched the sun sink towards the horizon, her mind numb, her heart empty. Leandro's words hammered relentlessly through her mind, her heart.

You seem like the kind of girl who takes what she can get when she can get it. Who enjoys the ride and damns the consequences. Who doesn't care…about anything.

He'd summed her up so pithily, condemned her so readily— and in many ways he was right. That *was* who she'd been, who she'd had to be—at least on the outside. Act as if you don't care—or, better yet, *really* don't care. Then you won't be hurt when it's time to move on, when Sheila decides she's had enough.

Don't cry, Zoe. The next place will be better…

And the next, and the next, and the next. There was always something better somewhere else. That had been her mother's maxim, and Zoe had taken it as her own. She'd never known another way to live, and it was a *safe* way to live—you kept your heart guarded and had no home or family, nothing to care about.

Except somehow now she did. She hadn't come to Italy to care. She'd come to escape, to forget Steve. And yet as she lay on her bed she realised Steve hardly mattered any more; he was no more than a smokescreen for the true feelings she had—feelings which scared her.

She cared.

She cared about Leandro, about the villa, about the charade of domesticity she'd been acting out in the last few days. For the first time in her life her home was more than a bedsit or a grotty hostel. Her life was more than a meaningless job.

How pathetic to think she'd found something here. Hadn't Leandro made it clear what he thought of her?

Yet it both saddened and angered her to think that he had all this—all that she'd never had—and he was throwing it away.

Zoe brushed at the tears she hadn't realised were falling, silently streaking down her face. Now, as dusk began to blanket the lake, causing long shadows to melt into each other, she fell into an uneasy doze.

When she awoke, disorientated and still drowsy, night had fallen, and the room was illuminated only by a sliver of moonlight. A shutter creaked and then banged shut in a gust of evening air—a haunting, lonely sound that propelled Zoe from her bedroom in search of some comfort, if not company.

She made her way downstairs, picking her way carefully through the dark, and found some more leftover pasta in the kitchen, eating it cold while standing by the sink.

She felt bruised all over—lonely and heartsore and just plain sad. Gazing out at the unending darkness—even the lake was empty of boats and their comforting lights due to the wind—she decided to retreat back to her bedroom. Then, on the bottom stair, she heard a noise from the drawing room.

She hesitated, her hand curling around the cold iron railing as she listened. It had been two sounds, she realised: the clink of crystal and the more human sound of a sigh.

Still she didn't move, weighing her options. Leandro had to be in there, alone. Did she want to see him? Talk to him?

Even as these thoughts and their implications flitted through her brain, she was already turning, drawn towards Leandro with the irresistible force of a magnet. With need. She hesitated for no more than half a second on the threshold—surely no good could come of this?—before pushing the door further open with her fingertips.

'Well, hello.'

Zoe stiffened at Leandro's unaccustomed drawl. The room was shrouded in darkness save for a single lamp in the corner, next to the chair he was sprawled in. His hair was rumpled, the top two buttons of his half-tucked shirt undone, and he held a tumbler of whisky in his hand.

Zoe hesitated, not sure how to handle Leandro like this. There was something sad, and even vulnerable about him, yet she refused to let her sympathy overcome her sense. His harsh words from this afternoon still reverberated in her mind, stung her soul, and even in the dim room she could see a dangerous glint in his eye.

'Hello,' she said a bit stiffly. 'What are you doing?'

Leandro cocked an eyebrow, and Zoe flushed. It was a stupid question. 'Isn't it obvious?' he said, lifting his glass. 'I'm drinking.'

'Drunk?' Zoe interjected, and Leandro laughed, a sound without humour.

'Not quite. Not yet.' He gestured to the half-empty bottle on the sideboard. 'Care to join me?'

'No, thank you.' Zoe knew she sounded prissy, but she didn't care. She didn't like Leandro in this mood—didn't know what he might say. What could happen.

'I thought you'd be good for at least one drink.'

'You thought a lot of things about me,' Zoe returned sharply.

'So I did.' Leandro turned his glass around in his hands, the lamplight making the whisky glint amber and gold. 'Are you trying to say they're not true?'

'Considering you summed me up as a mercenary trollop, then, yes, that *is* what I'm trying to say.' Zoe clenched her fists, her nails biting into her palms.

'Maybe I was too harsh,' Leandro replied musingly. 'But then so were you.'

'About what?'

He was silent, still rotating his glass between his palms, and after a moment Zoe wondered if he'd even heard the question. Then he looked up, and her breath came out in a soft rush at the sorrow in his eyes.

'You told me I was completely blinded by my past. That I'm spitting on my history, my family.'

He lapsed into silence again, his expression distant, and Zoe waited, caught between impatience and interest. And hope, strangely.

'I don't know why that disturbs me,' he finally said. He looked up at her again. '*You* disturb me.'

'I don't mean to.'

'Don't you? You're just like them, you know. At least I thought you were. Like all the others.'

He shook his head, and Zoe frowned. 'What do you mean, all the others?'

He brushed her question aside, setting his glass down on the table with a clatter before sweeping his arm to take in the shabby faded room, the whole villa. 'This villa was beautiful in its day. Do you know how long it's been in the Filametti family? Five hundred years. It was given to my ancestor by Ludovico Sforza, for his help in the wars against Venice and Florence. And my family held on to it through Spanish and Austrian domination, the Napoleonic wars, the devastation of the Fascist party. Through all of it we survived.'

He shook his head—whether in disbelief or something darker, Zoe couldn't tell.

'So, if your family managed to survive all that, why are you selling it now?' It was the obvious question, yet she still felt intrusive—insensitive—for asking it.

Leandro turned to look at her, and for a moment his eyes burned blue fire, pure rage. Then that brief light was extinguished, and he slumped back in his seat once more. 'I'm proud of my heritage,' he said. 'Despite what you think. That is why I'm so ashamed of what has happened.'

Zoe took a step into the room, and then another. 'What *has* happened?'

'The Filametti family was ruined,' Leandro replied simply, his voice more matter-of-fact than bleak. 'Completely ruined.'

CHAPTER SIX

THE statement seemed to have brought a new lucidity to Leandro, for he rose from the chair in one brisk yet fluid movement, and drained his glass before putting away the bottle of whisky.

Zoe watched him, unspeaking, not knowing what to say. There was a brittleness, she saw, to his movements; his face was averted from her. When he'd finished his tidying tasks he moved to the window, his back to her, his hands shoved deep into his pockets, and gazed out into the night.

'I used to play football out on the front lawn,' he said after a moment. 'My father loved the game. We played together.' He spoke in the same flat voice he'd been using all along, yet Zoe thought she heard a thread of wistfulness underneath, a ghost of memory.

She moved a bit closer to him, still wary and uncertain, treading dangerous, uncertain ground. 'And then?'

Lost in his own memories, Leandro didn't seem to hear her. Or perhaps he chose not to hear. He simply continued talking. 'We had parties in the summer, on the terrace. My sister and I used to hide under the tables and listen to the adults talking. They never said anything remotely interesting, though. There was always delicious food...*panettone, pastiocciotti*. We'd steal some when no one was looking.' He shook his head, and as Zoe drew closer to him she saw the glimmer of a smile on his face, although his eyes were hard. Unforgiving.

'And then?' she asked again, for she knew instinctively that this was the beginning of the story, not the end.

'Natale—Christmas—here was magical,' he continued, as if trying to explain something to her. Prove something, even. 'Candles in every window, a Yule log burning here in this room, and we'd walk to Midnight Mass in Lornetto. Once, even, there was snow. I tried to make a snowball, but it was no more than a dusting and it fell apart in my hands. My father laughed, and told me he would give me a snowball for Christmas. And he did. I don't know how he managed it—he must have sent someone to the mountains to collect snow. He hid it in the freezer and made a treasure hunt for me to find it.'

Leandro lapsed into silence and Zoe stood next to him, her heart aching. These were the kinds of memories she had always dreamed of, longed for, and from the taut set of Leandro's jaw she knew they were precious to him too. Precious and yet desecrated somehow—by what? What had happened to him? To his family?

She couldn't bring herself to ask, *And then?*

'It's those memories that I can't bear to lose. They matter more than all my so-called heritage.' He half turned to her, the faint smile now full-fledged, hard and cynical. 'Pathetic, really.'

'I don't think so,' Zoe said quietly. 'I'd love to have memories like that.'

'Would you? Even if what happened afterwards ruined everything—coloured it so it all seemed absurd and false?'

Zoe blinked at the ragged harshness in his voice. 'At least you *have* memories.'

'What are you saying?' Leandro demanded. 'You must have had parents—a family of some kind?'

'I had—have—a mother.' Zoe cut him off, her words flat.

Leandro stared at her for a moment before repeating her own question. 'And then?'

'I don't know who my father is,' Zoe told him. She felt heat rush up into her face and tried to control it. 'I don't think my mother does either.' She'd never told anyone this—never exposed the shaming paucity of her childhood. 'We didn't have a home—not a villa like this, not a house or apartment, not anything.'

Leandro frowned. 'What do you mean?'

Now Zoe found herself smiling just as cynically as he had.

'It's hard for you to imagine, isn't it, Leandro? You don't even realise the luxury you had growing up. I'm not even talking about wealth or prestige. I mean a family. Two parents, a sister—more for all I know.' She shook her head. 'Something normal.'

'It was far from normal,' Leandro cut in harshly.

'It sounds pretty wonderful to me,' Zoe challenged. 'Christmas, parties, football. It sounds like an American television show—happy families, Italian-style.'

'Well, as I soon found out, it wasn't.'

'No? What happened?' Zoe felt a flaring of anger, and it surprised her. Why did she care what had happened to Leandro's family? What he'd felt or done about it? Why did it matter to *her*?

Yet it did; she couldn't bear to see him throw it all away, no matter how bitter he was. He'd had something, something wonderful and he didn't even realise it, wouldn't acknowledge it.

'What happened,' Leandro said, his voice as sharp as broken glass, 'is my father gambled everything away. Lost it all—squandered it, even.'

'Like you're doing.'

The silence following her pronouncement was both chilling and profound. Leandro's eyes darkened, the skin around his mouth whitening with rage. 'Are you comparing me to my father?' he asked in a quiet, lethal voice, and Zoe knew that was the worst thing she could have done.

Still, her anger—as unreasonable as it might have been—fuelled her. 'There seem to be some similarities.'

Leandro's hand slashed through the air. 'I am nothing—*nothing* like my father!' His voice came out in a cry of desperation, a plea for mercy. 'Nothing like him,' he repeated in a savage whisper. His features twisted with regret, memory, fear.

'What did he do that was so terrible?' Zoe whispered.

Leandro was silent for so long, his face averted from her once more, that she wondered if he would ever answer. The room was dark save the one small circle of light from the delicate table lamp.

'Do you know why I hired you?' Leandro asked finally. His back was still to her, his voice was flat and unemotional, yet Zoe sensed the deep current of anger and disappointment underneath.

'You told me earlier today it was because I didn't know you,' she replied evenly. 'A perfect stranger, you said.'

'Yes. Exactly. I wanted someone who had never heard the name Filametti. Who hadn't seen my father and his trollops splashed across the tabloids. Who didn't see my family as either a tragedy or a laughing stock.'

'Well, you succeeded there,' Zoe replied, struggling to maintain a calm tone. Leandro's words were branding her brain: tragedy, *trollop*. 'I'd never heard of you.'

'Nearly everyone in Italy has,' Leandro replied diffidently. 'Georgio Filametti—my father—made sure of it. Oh, he was famous enough to begin with—although I don't think I realised it as a child. How could I? As a child you simply accept the way things are as the only way they can be. You don't know any different…or any better.'

'I suppose that in your case that was true,' Zoe replied, thinking it had certainly not been *her* situation. Even from a very young age she had been aware there was something unusual and even unnatural about her upbringing—her mother's frantic flitting from anonymous city to anonymous city, her confused and unhappy daughter in tow.

'He had everything going for him,' Leandro said, and now there was disgust in his voice. 'Related to royalty, Italy's golden child, adored and intelligent too. He could have accepted everything as his due, given to him on a golden plate, but he worked hard. He was in finance, banking, and he made his own money.'

'He sounds like a good man,' Zoe said after a moment, when Leandro lapsed into silence once more.

'I thought he was,' Leandro agreed, his voice caught between bitterness and grief. 'I *thought* he was. But he proved me—us—the whole of Italy wrong.'

Zoe kept silent. She could not imagine what Leandro's father had done that was so unbearably unforgivable. Then Leandro dragged in a breath and told her, each word spat out like a loathsome, poisonous confession.

'He lost it all,' he said. 'Gave it away. And for what? A few nights' sordid pleasure.' He glared at her in accusation, and Zoe recoiled. She didn't understand, but somehow this felt personal—as if Leandro were accusing *her*.

'What do you mean?' she asked, struggling to raise her voice above an uncertain whisper.

'My father was an addict of sorts,' Leandro explained coolly. 'Addicted to women—cheap women, mercenary women, glossy, but from the gutter all the same.'

'He had affairs?' Zoe clarified, and Leandro smiled mirthlessly.

'Oh, he didn't just have affairs. He had torrid, sordid, *pathetic* encounters. *He* was pathetic… Those women took him for everything he had. And I don't just mean his money. I mean his dignity, his self-respect. His business began to fail, he started embezzling, and then one of his paramours began blackmailing him. Eventually it all came crashing down—a grand exposé in the papers, grainy photos of everything.' Leandro's mouth twisted. 'And my father couldn't face it. So he ran away. Disappeared to Monaco with what was left of his money, and left my mother to face it all.'

'And you?' Zoe surmised softly. 'How old were you when this happened?'

Leandro looked surprised by the question. 'Thirteen,' he said shortly.

Thirteen. Zoe's heart ached. Almost a man, and yet such a child. 'And then?' she asked quietly.

Leandro shrugged. 'I haven't seen him since. My mother died two years ago, and she never saw him again either. He'd left her shamed, a virtual pauper, smeared and ridiculed in every newspaper, and yet she still couldn't hate him.'

Because you hated him enough already, Zoe finished silently. She shook her head. It was a sad story—a tragedy, just as Leandro had said—and yet it seemed to her all the more tragic that he was selling this villa, throwing away the few good memories he had.

'If your father lost everything, what happened to this villa?'

'It couldn't be lost,' Leandro replied. 'It was never his to begin with. It was my grandfather's, and when he died last year it passed to me. Of course no one had the funds to restore it—

my grandfather had spent all his money paying my father's debts. He managed to hold on to the villa only barely.'

'So the villa's ownership skipped over your father?'

Leandro smiled grimly. 'My grandfather made that provision in his will after my father showed his true colours. Chasing after every tart who took what she could get.'

Zoe nodded, digesting this even as another echo began its insistent, remorseless beating in her brain. *You seem like the kind of girl who takes what she can get when she can get it. Who enjoys the ride and damns the consequences. Who doesn't care...about anything.* Shock rippled icily through her, pooled like cold acid in her stomach. She was beginning to understand why this felt so personal.

'And you think I'm just like them?' she whispered, cruel comprehension making her feel sick, ashamed, though she knew she had nothing to be ashamed of. 'Your father's women—those heartless, blackmailing scum! You think I'm just like them. That's why...'

Dizzily she stepped back from him, reaching for a chair to steady her, her fingers curling slickly around the burnished wood. She didn't know why the realisation should hurt so much, should make her feel as if her heart was breaking. Her heart wasn't even involved. It *couldn't* be. Yet at that moment she felt as if someone had reached right down inside and wrenched it apart. She felt torn up inside, shattered into pieces...

It all made a kind of sickening sense now—why Leandro resisted his attraction to her, why he judged her so harshly.

I shouldn't...want...

He was afraid of becoming like his father, of *being* his father—risking and ruining everything for *a girl like her*. A tart, a trollop, a cold-hearted, *blackmailing*—

Bile rose in her throat and she choked it down, willing herself not to cry, not to care.

Wasn't that how she'd kept herself safe all these years? First as a child, losing best friends and favoured 'uncles' when her mother had decided it was time to move on, and then later, as an adult, when she'd followed in her mother's footsteps, quite literally, never staying long enough to know or be known, because she was afraid to try any other way. Afraid to be hurt.

Yet now she *was* hurt. Now she hurt all over.

Leandro turned slowly to look at her. There was a new, naked desolation in his face, a bleakness in his eyes that somehow seemed strangely vulnerable. 'No, Zoe,' he said quietly. 'I don't think that. You're not like them at all.'

Tears, treacherous tears, gathered at the corners of her eyes and she dashed at them angrily. 'But you said—'

'I think I was trying to prove to myself that you were. And you must admit you *do* project a certain image.' Leandro's sudden wry smile took the sting out of his words.

'Image…' Zoe repeated numbly. It was all about image. Who she pretended to be because it was safer. It wasn't who she really was—who she'd *ever* been.

'Is it just an image?' Leandro asked softly. 'Who are you really, Zoe Clark? Why did you come to Italy? What are you running away from? Because I am beginning to think you have secrets—perhaps as many as I do.'

Yes, she did. And the fact that he'd guessed made Zoe ache. She almost *wanted* him to know, to tell him all of it, to finally be known. Understood. Accepted.

Loved.

His hand reached out slowly, hypnotically, to brush a strand of hair away from her cheek. 'And,' he added, his voice lowered to a rasp, 'why can't I get you out of my mind?'

'I can't get you out of mine either,' Zoe admitted shakily.

They stared at each other, silent, still, and Zoe knew it was a moment for making decisions. For turning away if they could. And surely that was the safer, saner course of action? She already knew she was in way too deep—cared far too much. Yet she couldn't—didn't even want to. Under Leandro's penetrating stare she felt vulnerable, emotionally bare, and even though it terrified her it was something she wanted. Craved. To know and be known. *Finally.*

She didn't know who moved first, who gave in before the other. It didn't matter. One moment they were simply staring at one another, and the next they were a tangle of arms, of legs and lips and skin, seeking and finding again and again, like deep-water divers desperate for air.

She stumbled backwards, tripping on the frayed fringe of the carpet, and Leandro's arms came around her, steadying her. Holding her. She never wanted him to let her go.

She could feel him pressed against her, felt the hard length of his thigh, the chiselled muscles of his chest. Felt his lips on her skin, touching her bare shoulder, the nape of her neck, her jawbone. She shuddered under his caress, wanting more. Needing more.

There was nothing desperate or angry here; there was, instead, something precious. Something beautiful. Or so Zoe wanted to believe.

Her fingers threaded through Leandro's hair, drawing him closer. He kissed her again, deeply, drinking her in, and Zoe let him—let herself open to his touch in a way she never had before.

Leandro drew back, tilted her chin so she was forced to meet her gaze, and somehow it felt even more intimate than a kiss.

'Zoe…are you sure?'

Her heart thudding in her ears, desire coursing wildly through her veins, her senses alert and her thoughts blurred, there was nothing Zoe wanted more than to give a simple yes.

Yet as Leandro's gaze burned into hers she found that single word so difficult to say.

Yes. What was she agreeing to? A single night of pleasure? A one-night stand with her employer, who would walk away from her in the morning?

She was worth more than that. She *wanted* more than that.

'Zoe?' Leandro said softly, his fingers caressing her cheek. Such a light, simple touch, and yet it reached deep inside her—made her ache from its tenderness.

'Yes,' she whispered, praying she wouldn't regret her decision, knowing that when Leandro looked at her like that she was powerless to say anything else. To walk away, to stay safe. 'Yes, I'm sure.'

He led her by the hand, silent and accepting, through the

shadowy, moonlit corridors of the villa. Everything was hushed, as if even the house around them sensed the expectancy of the moment.

In his bedroom he stopped before the wide double bed with its navy sheets and turned slowly to her.

'Let me look at you.'

Zoe fidgeted under his sweeping gaze, the airy confidence she'd cloaked herself with falling away. Had anyone really looked at her before? Had anyone seen who she truly was? Had *she*?

Steve had, she supposed. He'd seen her naked. Yet this felt like so much more than a physical baring. She felt as if her senses, her soul, her whole self were being bared. Exposed. And the strange thing was that she didn't mind. She *wanted* it.

Slowly Leandro reached out and pushed the straps of her top off her shoulders. With the barest shrug the garment slithered off her, leaving her nearly naked save a skimpy pair of pyjama shorts. Zoe felt goosebumps rise on her arms even though she wasn't cold. Leandro was still looking at her, and she fought not to cover herself, to stand there proud and bold, willing to be vulnerable.

He reached out to stay the arm she hadn't realised was already moving closer, protectively, towards her body.

'Don't. You're beautiful.'

'So are you,' she admitted with a little smile, and then reached out to lift his tee shirt over his head and shoulders. He shrugged it away completely and she let her hands drift down his bare chest. His muscles flexed under her touch.

'What you do to me,' he murmured. 'I've been helpless to resist you since I first saw you on my doorstep.'

'And that infuriated you?' Zoe whispered, her hands resting on his belt buckle.

Leandro helped her to unclasp it. Such a simple task. Yet she felt as shy and uncertain as the virgin she almost was—for even though she'd had a physical relationship she'd never felt like this.

'Yes,' he replied. 'I didn't want to want you. But I did. God knows, I did.'

'And now?' She shouldn't ask the question, shouldn't be so desperate for its answer.

'I *do*.' He pulled her towards him, her breasts colliding against his chest, and murmured against her hair, 'Can't you tell?'

Yes, she could. But she wondered at the war that had raged within Leandro. Would he hate her in the morning? Hate himself? Could she stand it?

His hands stroked her body, reached up to cup her breasts with sleek yet gentle movements that still managed to stir her up inside, and it was all too easy to push away that scared little voice and give herself up to feeling. Feeling wanted, desired. Treasured, even.

She wouldn't think about the morning.

Yet morning came, as Zoe had known it would. She lay in Leandro's arms as dawn crept along the horizon, sent its pale pink fingers streaking along the floor. A gentle breeze rustled the curtains. She'd been awake most of the night, caught between regret and wonder. It was an uncomfortable place.

Her body still tingled and ached from their lovemaking; Leandro had touched and caressed her with an intimacy that even now astounded her. He'd touched her everywhere, fingers and lips seeking, exploring, yet it hadn't simply been about the physical pleasure, amazing and intense as that had been. It had been something more, something deeper, and she'd seen it reflected in Leandro's eyes. This wasn't the one-night stand they'd both silently agreed on.

She'd seen it in Leandro's eyes when she'd touched him, felt it when he'd shuddered and almost—*almost*—tried to resist her caress. As if he'd been afraid it was too much. Too intense, too wonderful.

They were both afraid, Zoe had realised with a thrill of understanding as she'd traded caress for caress with Leandro. They were both protecting themselves, trying not to care, and yet now it was all stripped away.

When he'd finally entered her it had felt like the purest form of communication.

Yet now, as sunlight slanted across the floor and Leandro slept next to her, the doubts crept in. Last night she'd never felt so physically vulnerable, so emotionally exposed. Or was she just feeling that way now? Lying in his arms, waiting for him to wake up, having no idea what the expression on his face would be?

Disgust? Desire? Indifference? Irritation? The range of possibilities was frightening. Zoe had never felt so hesitant, so uncertain, and she knew why. She wasn't in control. She hadn't played it safe.

She'd let herself care.

CHAPTER SEVEN

LEANDRO lay on his side and watched Zoe sleep. It was an hour or so past dawn and she looked exhausted. Her lashes fanned on her cheeks, shadows showed under her eyes, yet she was still so beautiful.

His gut tightened—and so did something a little higher, a little more vital and frightening. His heart.

How had he come to care for this woman?

He meant what he'd said last night; he knew she wasn't like the women his father had chased after. Those women had been grasping, shallow, obvious. Zoe might only be after a good time, but Leandro knew she was far from the greedy blackmailer he'd been determined to see her as. He thought of her taking such simple pleasure in buying peaches, serving *biscotti*. She was a woman who in her unguarded moments looked thoughtful and even sad, and he knew she'd never been the schemer he'd wanted to believe her to be.

Gently he brushed a tendril of hair away from her forehead and she sighed softly in her sleep. Leandro smiled at the sound. What was she hiding? he wondered. He thought of her guarded references to an unhappy past—a lack of home and family—and wondered just what had made Zoe Clark determined to treat the world with such insouciant indifference.

Determined not to care, as he was determined not to care.

His gut clenched again, and so did his heart. It was a warning, a reminder that Leandro could not afford to ignore. He couldn't afford to get involved.

He knew what happened when you did. He knew how much it hurt.

Determinedly he pushed away the wave of desire—and, more fearfully, something deeper—and rolled away from Zoe, vainly searching once more for sleep.

Zoe realised she must have finally fallen into a doze, for when she awoke the sun was high in the sky and Leandro was still sleeping—although now his back was to her. Even in the ignorance of sleep it felt like a rejection, and Zoe tried to prepare herself for the dreaded morning-after conversation. Confrontation, more like.

As if Leandro had sensed her thoughts, he stirred and slowly rolled over, blinking sleep out of his eyes only for a second before he was instantly alert.

'Good morning.'

His tone was expressionless, impossible to discern, and it gave Zoe no clue as to how she should behave. She gave a little smile that could mean anything—or nothing—and tossed her hair out of her eyes, drawing the sheet protectively over her in a casual gesture that Leandro still noticed.

'Good morning.'

They stared at each other, silent and unblinking, for a long moment, before Leandro smiled lazily and said, 'How about some breakfast?'

So there was to be no conversation. No confrontation. At least not yet. Zoe didn't know whether to feel disappointed or relieved. She stretched sleepily to mask her confusion, buy herself time. She didn't know how to act—couldn't afford to be honest. Didn't even know what honesty would look like, sound like. Her feelings for Leandro were so new, raw and untested. She was afraid to try them out and see if they were real.

'All right,' she said after a moment, and slipped quickly from the bed, throwing on her discarded clothes with her back to Leandro. Still she felt him watching, and a rosy blush spread over her whole body.

When she turned around again, Leandro had pulled on his

pyjama bottoms. His chest was still magnificently bare. Zoe averted her gaze, feeling awkward and gauche.

'I'll let you off the hook this morning,' he said. 'I'll cook breakfast.'

He was as good as his word, and as Zoe sat at the kitchen table, sipping coffee, Leandro cracked half a dozen eggs into a bowl and began to briskly whisk them.

'I can't make much,' he told her, 'but I can do a decent omelette.'

'Sounds good,' Zoe replied lightly.

And it smelled good too, when, a few minutes later, Leandro placed an omelette in front of her, steaming and fragrant with basil and tomato.

He sat across from her and handed her a fork. 'Dig in.'

They ate silently for a few moments, the sun streaming through the wide windows, glinting off the lake. It should have been a pleasant, comfortable, even happy moment, yet Zoe could only feel the tension uncoiling in her belly, wrapping around her heart.

What is this? she wanted to ask. *What are we?* A one-night stand? A summer fling?

Was she actually thinking it might be more?

She choked on a bite of omelette and reached desperately for her half-drunk mug of coffee. Leandro watched her in concern. When she'd recovered herself, she found she had a bit courage as well, and she set her mug down with careful determination.

'So…'

Leandro sat back in his chair, his arms folded, as if he'd expected this. 'So?'

His expression was guarded, yet not unfriendly. Neutral, Zoe decided, which could mean—or could hide—anything.

She licked her lips, her mouth and throat suddenly dry, the words she'd intended to speak evaporating into thin air. 'What do you want, Leandro?' she finally asked. 'From me?' And then she held her breath and waited. Worse—hoped.

For what?

Leandro was silent for a long moment. He raked a hand through his hair, let out a long sigh. Not good signs. 'We had a good time last night, Zoe.'

Something in Zoe wilted. Withered. *A good time.* That was all she was good for, the kind of girl she still was. To him, at least. Inside she didn't feel like that at all.

'Yes,' she agreed, and reached for her mug once more, desperate to disguise the disappointment she felt rolling through her in consuming waves. Surely Leandro would be able to see it in her eyes, her face? 'Yes, we did,' she repeated, her voice stronger now. She was able to meet his gaze directly.

'So?' Leandro shrugged, smiling a bit. 'You're here for… what…? Another two months?'

'So we can have two months of good times,' Zoe filled in for him, feeling sick.

Leandro frowned, and Zoe saw something crystallise and harden in his eyes. 'Is that not what *you* want? You seem like you'd…' He trailed off, shrugging, and Zoe forced herself to smile.

'I know what I seem like.'

'I'm not judging you,' Leandro told her quickly. 'You know that?'

Zoe nodded slowly. 'Yes.' And he wasn't—not really. She was judging herself. She rose from the table, clearing the plates—mindless tasks, because she couldn't think, didn't *want* to think, about how she was feeling. How much she hurt.

'Zoe…' Leandro rose as well. 'I feel as if I've said something to offend you.'

'Offend me? No, of course not.' She leaned against the sink, a damp dish towel in one hand. 'Like you said, we had a good time last night, Leandro. There's no reason for it to stop, is there?' She swallowed, forced herself to continue. 'As long as we know what to expect, no one gets hurt—right?'

'Right,' Leandro agreed slowly. He didn't move, and Zoe turned determinedly back to the dishes. When he spoke again his voice was low and final. 'If you were expecting…more, I'm afraid I don't have it to give, Zoe.'

'Why should I expect more?' she asked, her back to him. She heard the brittleness in her voice, felt it inside.

'It's not about who *you* are,' Leandro said. He crossed the room in a few long steps and reached out to stay her arm, his fingers curling around her wrist, burning her bare skin. 'It's who *I* am.'

Zoe's fingers clenched around the dish towel. She looked down, blinked hard. 'I see.'

'Do you? Do you remember when I said I didn't plan to marry or have children? Any of that?'

Blink again. Quickly. 'Yes.'

'I meant that. I'm not—' He shrugged, releasing her arm. 'After everything, I'm not capable of that. And I didn't think you wanted it either.'

He had said as much. Not her. Yet she wasn't about to point that out now. 'No, not really,' she said instead. She pushed her hair back from her face and found a smile. 'We've had a good time, Leandro, like you said. And there's no reason why it can't continue.' Except for the fact that her heart was splintering apart at every damning word he said.

'All right, then.' Leandro smiled, and then drew her into his arms.

Zoe went, unresisting, recognising her own shaming powerlessness. He kissed her once, deeply and sweetly, and her splintered heart seemed to squeeze together again, still hoping—

Then he released her.

'I'll see you later, then. I need to do some work.'

Mutely Zoe nodded and watched him leave, thinking sadly that he was always the first to go.

Too distracted and weary to start on her own work, she took a second mug of coffee out onto the terrace and sat curled in a chair, gazing blindly at the lake now full of sailboats and pleasure yachts. Above her there was the steady clatter and hammer of the roofers, working hard to make sure Leandro could sell his villa.

His home.

Except he refused to think of it as a home—didn't *want* a home. And with a growing sense of desolation Zoe realised what that meant for her.

She wanted a home. She wanted a family. Children, love, laughter, safety, warmth. She wanted it all, and she wanted it with Leandro.

Her mouth twisted cynically. How could she fall in love so

quickly, so hopelessly? How could she want something so impossible—as impossible as the neat little houses with their window boxes and lace curtains that she'd seen from the window of a bus, *en route* to another town, another adventure. She'd drawn them secretly on scraps of paper and crumpled them up before her mother saw, knowing she would pour scorn on those dreams.

She should crumple up these new dreams too—hide them away before Leandro could guess her true feelings. He'd be horrified, she knew, to realise just how much she wanted from him. Even if he no longer thought of her as an unscrupulous tart, he probably still considered her to be the kind of girl who enjoyed whatever came her way for a time, and then moved on.

And that was the kind of girl she was—whether she liked it or not. The kind of girl she would have to be.

Zoe took a sip of coffee; it had grown cold. She knew she would accept Leandro's offer, take what she could get even though she wanted so much more. It would simply have to be enough.

Leandro stared at the letter on his desk, the crabbed writing, barely legible, and felt a wave of disgust roll over him, tinted— *tainted*—by the faintest trace of pity.

Too little, too late. He wasn't remotely ready to forgive. He never would be.

He pushed the letter aside, raking a hand through his hair before dropping it to his side. It wasn't just the letter that was making him feel restless; it was Zoe.

Their conversation this morning, meant to put everything on a neat, clear footing, had left him instead with a deepening sense of unease and dissatisfaction.

It wasn't enough.

It would have to be.

Last night, he acknowledged with the flicker of a smile, had been wonderful. Wonderful was too simplistic a word; it had been…transcendent. His smile deepened cynically; he was sounding like some lovesick poet.

Yet he couldn't deny that last night had changed him, touched him in a way he'd never expected. There had been an openness, an honesty to their lovemaking he'd never experienced with another woman. As if they had not just been baring their bodies, but their souls. And joining them as one.

Leandro let out a sigh of sardonic disgust. Really, he was sounding positively fanciful. The truth was, he hadn't been with a woman in a long time, and the enforced intimacy of the villa had created a false sense of—what?

Connection? Closeness? *Love?*

Leandro snorted again and pushed away from his desk. He couldn't work, but neither did he want to think about Zoe. She occupied too much of his mind already.

He'd enjoy their liaison for a few months more, and then he'd leave. So would she. Easier for everyone. Easier and safer. The best thing, really, and Leandro almost—almost—believed it.

Zoe didn't see Leandro for the rest of the day, which passed with a sorrowful, aching slowness. She was eager to see him again, yet she also dreaded it.

Wasn't this what she'd always tried to avoid? This hopeless disappointment? People left. Either they did or you did. No one stayed for long.

Still, Zoe told herself with brisk determination, she had over two months. Leandro had offered her that much, and she would take it and enjoy it.

It was dusk when he found her, attempting to grill two chicken breasts. She peered into the massive oven, which was ominously dark and cool.

'Something's gone wrong, I think,' she said, as Leandro came up behind her. She felt a little frisson of surprise as his arms slipped around her waist and he kissed her neck, sending even more frissons rippling up and down her spine.

'Has the oven finally given up the ghost? It is old—at least thirty years. Our cook, Maria, used to complain of it. She had a love-hate relationship with that thing.'

'I can understand why.' For a brief moment Zoe let herself lean back against the hard plane of Leandro's chest, allowed herself the luxury of relaxing into his arms, of feeling safe and loved.

'Never mind about the oven,' Leandro murmured against her hair. 'Let me take you out to a proper restaurant. Somewhere in Como, maybe.'

His arms tightened around her, his hands sliding along her ribcage. Zoe felt a trembling thrill of desire at the easy caress. 'Are you sure you don't want to stay here?'

'Well, now that you mention it…' His voice rumbled with suppressed laughter. 'Still, there is time. Let me take you out, Zoe.'

And it was so wonderfully, pitifully easy to say yes.

She slipped on a sundress in a pale, shimmering lavender, added a spangled shawl and strappy sandals and she was ready.

Leandro had changed into a suit of dark blue Italian silk, and he looked devastating. Zoe could hardly believe he was hers.

For just over two months. She must never forget that. Even if now it felt like for ever. She took his hand and he led her through the darkened gardens to the boat. They sped through the darkness, arriving at Como's dock in less than half an hour.

Leandro moored the boat and then helped her up. His fingers remained twined with hers all the way to the restaurant.

It was a small, intimate, expensive place—the kind of restaurant that only had half a dozen items on the menu, but all were sinfully delicious. They shared *tiramisu* for dessert, Leandro's eyes dark and heavy-lidded in the candlelight, and then he led her back to the boat.

It was magical being on the lake at night, with the smooth surface of the water reflecting the stars above. Leandro cut the motor so they drifted in the middle of the lake, the only sound the lap of the water against the sides of the boat. Zoe stood up, her hands curling around the railing. A slight breeze rippled her hair, and she pulled her shawl around her shoulders.

'I love it here,' she said quietly. 'A night like this…I never want it to end.'

Behind her Leandro stiffened slightly, and too late Zoe realised what she had said—how it had sounded. She opened her mouth to take back the words, then closed it again. Let Leandro make of it what he would.

His hands came up to her shoulders, slipping under her gauzy wrap to warm her skin. 'A night like this need never end,' he said softly, and kissed the nape of her neck. Zoe shivered. 'Zoe…'

He pressed against her, her name a supplication and a thanksgiving. Zoe leaned back, her arms reaching up to twine around his neck, and for a split second she remembered the couple she'd watched with such bitter envy on the boat.

Now she was like them, happy and loved. For a time.

Banishing the thought, she turned so she could embrace Leandro fully, her lips seeking his, her body needing the caress, the release, yet her heart still wanting so much more.

The days slid by all too quickly; July melted into August. Zoe tried not to count, not to think of it. She refused to register the passing of the weeks, or the fact that the roofers were nearly done. She simply wanted to enjoy, to revel in Leandro's attention, in the nights in his bed, the days in his company.

They'd fallen into a routine of sorts, both working most of the morning before coming to the kitchen to share a coffee. Zoe was surprised at how easy it was to talk with him, to laugh and chat and speak of simple things, with the sunlight slanting through the wide, high windows.

They'd mostly return to work after lunch—although almost as often they'd find themselves upstairs, in bed, whiling away the lazy summer afternoons, loving each other.

In the evenings they often stayed in; Zoe would cook a meal they'd enjoy on the terrace, and then they'd curl up on one of the sofas in the drawing room and read or chat or even play chess. Leandro, laughing, had taught her, and was amazed at how quickly she'd picked up the game.

It felt, Zoe thought, as if they were reclaiming the villa. The past. Filling the rooms with laughter again, with love. For she loved Leandro—loved him with a completeness that cast out fear and left only a strong, happy certainty. She even let herself hope—believe—that he felt it too.

How could he lie with her in his arms night after night and not feel it? How could he swim and laugh and dance with her and not be in love?

She even let herself daydream—something she was usually wary of. She pictured the rooms of the villa restored and decorated again, filled with family. Their children, even.

Dangerous, Zoe knew, to want this much. To hope this much. Yet she couldn't help it. She was happy, and happiness did that to you. It made you believe.

For a little while, anyway.

The day the roofers finished up and left was cold and grey and drizzly. Zoe plied them with cups of coffee and freshly made *biscotti*, not wanting them to go. Not wanting to admit that it was all inexorably coming to an end.

Eventually they left, and she stood on the portico—a mason had repaired the crumbling step—and watched their van disappear down the drive, past the new red and white sign stuck to the iron gate.

A chill that was far colder than the needling drizzle swept through Zoe. The sign read *'Per La Vendita'*. For sale.

Zoe gazed at it for a moment, unblinking, as the coldness penetrated her bones, her heart, made her shiver deep inside. Of course she'd always known Leandro planned to sell the villa. She'd expected it, and yet…she hadn't. Somehow she'd managed to convince herself it wasn't really going to happen.

The drizzle strengthened to a downpour, and Zoe realised she was getting soaked. She turned back inside.

A glance at the calendar by the kitchen telephone told her it was the end of August. She could hardly believe it; they'd been lovers since the beginning of the summer. Her plane ticket was booked for next week.

Zoe sank into a kitchen chair and dropped her head into her hands, her mind buzzing. One week. Seven days. That was all she had left.

It's not enough. Her mind screamed it, her heart begged for more. And sitting there, alone in the kitchen, as the rain streamed down the windowpanes and turned the lake to no more than a dank grey mist, she realised she was going to get it. More. At least she was going to ask.

She'd even hope for an answer. The right answer. The belief

that Leandro loved her even if he didn't want to admit it to himself. Even if it didn't feel safe.

She rose from the table, her mind still buzzing, a strange new courage fizzing through her. That courage took her all the way to Leandro's study door, and after a second's hesitation she knocked. There was no answer. Another second and she turned the knob, opening the door with careful slowness.

The room was empty.

She'd only been in Leandro's study a handful of times; he told her he'd clean it himself, as he didn't want his papers disturbed. Looking at the messy scattering of papers across the desk's burnished mahogany top, Zoe wondered how they could be *more* disturbed.

She walked slowly around the room, taking in the masculine leather chairs, the bookshelves lined with dusty, musty tomes. This must have been his father's study, she realised, and wondered why Leandro had chosen it for himself. Punishment or retribution?

There were so many papers on the desk, some even scattered on the floor, that she didn't know why one small crumpled ball on top of the wastebasket intrigued her. She couldn't explain why she reached down to take it, laid it on the desk to smooth out the wrinkles. Perhaps because it had been more crumpled than the rest—savagely twisted into the tiniest ball possible. She remembered doing that with her own childish drawings. This was something no one must see, yet she couldn't bear to destroy it completely. Silently she scanned the single sheet; it was a letter, written in Italian. She could only understand a few phrases. They were enough.

Il più caro Leandro… Sono così spiacente… Lascilo vederlo… Il vostro padre votato…

Dearest Leandro… I'm so sorry… Let me see you… Your devoted father.

Leandro's father. He'd written him, after all these years, and Leandro had clearly thrown the letter away. Zoe stared at the words, trying to make more sense of it. The picture Leandro had painted of his father had been of an entirely unscrupulous man, corrupted by lust and driven by desperation. A man who had abandoned his family without a single backward glance, never to see them again.

Yet this letter showed a man who longed for forgiveness, for healing. Leandro, it seemed, was determined not to give it.

'What are you doing?'

Zoe looked up, tensing at Leandro's harsh voice—a voice he hadn't used with her for weeks. Months. It was, she knew, the voice of a judgemental stranger.

She also knew how it looked. She'd been snooping in Leandro's study, going through his rubbish and reading his personal letters. A blush rose from her throat to stain her cheeks. She pushed the letter away, as if to distance herself from it.

'I'm sorry.'

Leandro cocked one eyebrow, his mouth curling into an unpleasantly cynical smile. 'Are you? What for, Zoe?' He moved closer, with soft, lethal grace, and Zoe had to keep herself from taking a defensive step backwards.

'I—I was looking for you,' she said, stumbling over the simple explanation. 'I thought you'd be in here…'

'But I wasn't,' Leandro finished softly. 'So you decided to snoop around.'

He was so close to her now, his eyes bright with an anger Zoe didn't even understand. 'I'm sorry,' she said again. 'I didn't mean to snoop. I don't even know why I read that letter…'

'What?' His eyebrows rose in disbelief. 'You didn't read them all?'

'No!' Zoe shook her head, her hair brushing against her face. 'Leandro, why are you being so…so…?' She stopped, not wanting to finish the question. So cold. So hateful. So unforgiving.

'Why were you snooping, Zoe?' Leandro asked, in a voice no less hard for its softness. 'What were you looking for? My chequebook? My bank balance? A few bits and baubles?'

'What?' It took a full thirty seconds for comprehension to trickle coldly through her, while Leandro watched with scornful assurance. 'You think I was…? You still think I'm like one of your father's bimbos?'

Leandro cursed and turned away. 'No…of course not… I don't know what to think!'

The last came out in a cry of anguish, and Zoe grabbed the letter and shoved it towards him. He caught it reflexively against his chest, glancing down at the lines of scrawled writing, his brow furrowed.

'I was reading *this*,' she said heavily. 'A letter from your father. I can't understand all the Italian, but I know enough to realise he's sorry and he wants to see you.'

Leandro's fingers tightened around the wrinkled paper before, with deliberate, supreme indifference, he crumpled the letter once more and tossed it back in the bin. 'So?'

'*So?*' Zoe shook her head. 'Leandro, this is your *father*—your family.' She glanced at the crumpled ball of paper and felt all her hopes blow away like insubstantial dust. It had been such a deliberate dismissal of his father, his family, *everything*. Everything she'd begun to believe. 'You're never going to change, are you?'

'Change?' Leandro's voice sharpened, his eyes narrowing. 'Why should I change?'

'I thought…' Tears welled at the corners of her eyes, and only with effort could she blink them back. She felt disappointment and something deeper pouring through her, scalding her. She'd been so utterly foolish. 'I thought you'd change,' she finally said, and heard the ache of longing in her own voice. 'I thought you were changing—that what we had together…' She shook her head, not wanting to articulate just how deluded she had been. 'But I realise now I was wrong.'

'Yes, you were.' Leandro's voice was cold. 'I told you how much I had to give, Zoe. I never deceived you. I thought you were like—'

'Like you. Yes, I know.' She gave a tired imitation of a laugh and felt the tears sting her eyes again. 'But you see, I've come to realise this summer that I'm not really like that. I'm not sure I ever was. I know how I acted, how I wanted to be seen, but inside…' She shrugged. 'I want what I never had growing up. My mother was just like me. More, even. We travelled from place to place and we never stayed long—a few months at most—before she'd get itchy feet and have to pack up and leave. Always a new adventure, new school, new friends. Except they never really were friends—we never had time. I suppose I grew used to it, and I convinced myself that was how I wanted to live *my* life. Safer, really. You never get hurt, because no one ever gets close enough.'

A muscle ticked in Leandro's jaw, and for a moment he looked as if he might speak. But the silence just stretched on, endless, agonising. Zoe forced herself to continue.

'But now I know what I want, Leandro, and it's not just a good time. I don't even think I've ever *had* a good time—you were only my second lover, you know. I'm not the girl you thought I was. I'm not the girl *I* thought I was.'

'Zoe—'

Leandro broke off, and Zoe knew whatever he wanted to say he couldn't. He was right; he didn't have any more to give. He couldn't give her what she wanted—which was everything.

'I don't want a good time, Leandro. I want a home, a family. Love.' Her smile curled the corners of her mouth. 'I want it all, Leandro. And I thought maybe you did too…with me. I thought that even if you felt you didn't have enough to give you'd still want more. But you don't.'

Leandro was staring at her, his face horribly expressionless, making Zoe feel even more vulnerable. She'd exposed more to this man than anyone else, and he didn't even want it. *Her.*

'It's funny,' she finally said, breaking the taut, uncomfortable silence. 'It took a letter from your father to make me wake up from the dream I was living in. Because this was all a dream, wasn't it? Living here together like it's a home…our home…' Her voice cracked and she swallowed down the howl of sorrow that threatened to erupt out of her. 'If my father ever wrote to me like that I wouldn't throw away the letter. I'd keep it, and I'd see him. Because no matter what he did, Leandro, he's sorry now, and he loves you—'

'You can tell all that from a few badly translated lines of Italian?' Leandro's voice rang with contempt. 'You have no idea, Zoe.'

Zoe gazed at him, at his powerful frame and blazing eyes radiating scorn and rage, and she shook her head. 'Nor do you. Consider this my notice.'

Ducking her head so he couldn't see the tears that had begun to slip silently down her cheeks, she hurried out of the room.

Leandro watched her go, his chest aching as if he'd run a marathon, as if his heart were breaking.

But of course it wasn't. He didn't love Zoe Clark; he didn't love anybody. He'd made sure of that.

He cursed under his breath, wishing he'd never hired her, never met her, never loved her—

No. He did *not* love her. They'd been having a perfectly fine time, a *good* time, and she'd ruined it with silly schoolgirl dreams he'd thought her too savvy to possess.

I want it all. A home, family, love.

Didn't she realise those were all illusions? They didn't last, even if they were real in the first place. His had been torn apart by his father's lust and deceit, and she expected him to *forgive*?

Leandro cursed again. He would *never* forgive his father—no matter how many letters he wrote. He'd never allow him back in his life, his heart—

Or anyone?

The little voice that whispered inside him wasn't sly, only sad.

Leandro slumped in the chair behind his father's desk. A sudden memory pierced him with its sweetness: climbing on his father's lap while golden sunlight streamed through the window, playing with his pens and papers. His father had only chuckled, never minded, never swatted at his hands or told him to leave.

Not as he'd told Zoe to leave.

His father had always had time for him, always listened and loved him, and when he'd walked away that was what had hurt most of all.

Was he going to do the same? Prove once and for all he was just like his father—at least in that?

As the grey day turned to darkness, Leandro felt a fresh sorrow wash over him and he closed his eyes in regret.

* * *

In the end it was all too easy to creep out of the villa with her one beat-up bag. She left a note on the kitchen counter, asking for her last pay cheque to be sent to a postal box she kept in New York. Leandro's study door was firmly shut, and Zoe decided against knocking. There was nothing more to say; it had all, sadly, been said.

She walked down the driveway in a twilit drizzle, hitched her way to Menaggio, and then caught a bus to Milan. A few hours of waiting for a standby flight, and less than twenty-four hours after her confrontation with Leandro she was home.

Home. Home was hardly the word for the hostel she'd found in New York City's Meatpacking distract. It was a grotty room with a single bed, a battered bureau and a cracked sink. After the warmth and beauty of the villa, crumbling as it had been, it seemed all the more appalling—yet it was within Zoe's budget.

The next morning she took a newspaper and a red pen to a local diner, and over coffee and scrambled eggs began circling ads. Chambermaids, temp work, anonymous dead-end jobs. Her usual.

Yet after a few minutes she set the pen and newspaper aside and took a sip of her cooling coffee. She didn't want to do this any more.

Yet she didn't know what else to do; how did you begin finding a life for yourself? She'd taken a chance once and it hadn't paid off. Tears leaked out of the corners of her eyes and she blew on her coffee, trying to distract herself. She didn't want to burst into tears in the middle of a grimy diner.

'You're the devil to find.'

Zoe stilled, tensed, unable to believe the voice she was hearing. Then she looked up slowly and blinked. Twice. Leandro didn't disappear.

He was dressed in jeans and a shirt, sporting a full two days' growth of beard. He looked wonderful. He couldn't be real.

Yet he was.

'What are you doing here?' Zoe asked when she'd finally found her voice. Her heart was beginning to thump with loud, painful hope.

'Looking for you. I had no idea you'd run out on me so quickly.'

'You made it clear that you didn't want what I wanted,' Zoe

said quietly. She felt the tears again, and one trickled shamefully down her cheek.

'I did, didn't I?' Leandro agreed. He gestured to the vinyl seat across from Zoe. 'May I?' he asked, and when she nodded, slid into the booth.

Leandro was silent for a long moment, and a waitress sauntered over to take his order with a loud crack of her gum.

'I'll have what she's having,' Leandro said, and when the woman had left them alone he confessed in a voice so low Zoe could barely hear it, 'Zoe, I was afraid.'

'Afraid?' she whispered.

'You were right. It is safer to keep your distance. To never let anyone in. That's how I've been living my life since my father left, but somehow someone got in anyway. And I didn't realise how close until she was gone.'

'*How* close?' Zoe asked in a whisper, and Leandro smiled.

'Close enough to make me realise how many mistakes I was making, letting bitterness and fear guide me instead of love.'

Love. One simple, wonderful word. Zoe's heart ached. 'Love?' she repeated, and heard the longing in her voice.

'I love you, Zoe.' Leandro's voice was steady and strong. 'You've shown me so much…given me so much…and I almost threw it all away.' He reached across the table and brushed another tear from her cheek. 'I don't mean to make you cry.'

'I don't want to cry,' Zoe admitted with a choked laugh, two more tears streaking down her cheeks. 'I want to believe…'

'Believe me. I spent a great deal of time thinking yesterday, while I thought you were still in the villa. If I'd known how quickly you were going to leave—' Leandro shrugged ruefully. 'But, no. I needed that time. I suppose I'm a slow learner.'

'And what have you learned?'

'To forgive. To let go. To love.' Leandro's smile was endearingly crooked. 'I wrote to my father. I took down the "For Sale" sign. And I came to find you.'

Zoe's heart felt as if it was being squeezed even as it expanded with hope and joy. 'I can't believe you found me.'

'It took a lot of money,' Leandro told her wryly. 'I greased quite a few palms, trying to find what flight you'd taken, and then what address you'd given the cabbie. But in the end…I'm here.'

Zoe swallowed. 'Yes, you are.'

'And, frankly, I'd rather be somewhere else.' Her eyes widened and Leandro smiled. 'I'd rather be home,' he said softly. 'With you. Will you come home with me, Zoe? As my wife?'

Home. Wife. Words she'd never thought to hear, to hope for. Zoe could barely see Leandro through the shimmery haze of tears, yet she knew that the hardness was gone from his eyes, the bitterness and anger had melted away. There was only love shining there, perfect and true.

Home.

She reached across the table to twine her fingers with his. 'Yes,' she whispered, and knew there was no other place she'd rather be.

* * * * *

Bestselling Harlequin Presents® author

Lynne Graham

introduces

VIRGIN ON HER WEDDING NIGHT

Valente Lorenzatto never forgave Caroline Hales's
abandonment of him at the altar. But now he's
made millions and claimed his aristocratic Venetian
birthright—and he's poised to get his revenge.
He'll ruin Caroline's family by buying out their
company and throwing them out of their mansion...
unless she agrees to give him the wedding night
she denied him five years ago....

**Available May 2010
from Harlequin Presents!**

www.eHarlequin.com

HP12915

HARLEQUIN® *Blaze*™

is proud to introduce…

New York Times bestselling author

Brenda Jackson

with
SPONTANEOUS

Kim Cannon and Duan Jeffries have a great thing going.
Whenever they meet up, the passion between them
is hot, intense…spontaneous. And things really heat
up when Duan agrees to accompany her to her
mother's wedding. Too bad there's something
he's not telling her.…

Don't miss the fireworks!

*Available in May 2010
wherever Harlequin Blaze books are sold.*

red-hot reads

www.eHarlequin.com

HB79542

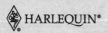
HARLEQUIN®

INTRIGUE®

BESTSELLING
HARLEQUIN INTRIGUE® AUTHOR

DELORES
FOSSEN

PRESENTS AN ALL-NEW
THRILLING TRILOGY

TEXAS MATERNITY:
HOSTAGES

When masked gunmen take over the maternity ward at a San Antonio hospital, local cops, FBI and the scared mothers can't figure out any possible motive. Before long, secrets are revealed, and a city that has been on edge since the siege began learns the truth behind the negotiations and must deal with the fallout.

LOOK FOR

THE BABY'S GUARDIAN, *May*
DEVASTATING DADDY, *June*
THE MOMMY MYSTERY, *July*

www.eHarlequin.com

HI69472

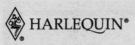
HARLEQUIN®

American ★ Romance®

LAURA MARIE ALTOM

The Baby Twins

Stephanie Olmstead has her hands full raising her twin baby girls on her own. When she runs into old friend Brady Flynn, she's shocked to find herself suddenly attracted to the handsome airline pilot! Will this flyboy be the perfect daddy— or will he crash and burn?

Babies & Bachelors USA

"LOVE, HOME & HAPPINESS"

www.eHarlequin.com

HAR75309

Stay up-to-date on all your romance-reading news with the brand-new Harlequin *Inside Romance!*

The Harlequin *Inside Romance* is a **FREE** quarterly newsletter highlighting our upcoming series releases and promotions!

Click on the *Inside Romance* link on the front page of
www.eHarlequin.com
or e-mail us at
InsideRomance@Harlequin.ca
to sign up to receive
your FREE newsletter today!

You can also subscribe by writing to us at: HARLEQUIN BOOKS
Attention: Customer Service Department
P.O. Box 9057, Buffalo, NY 14269-9057

Please allow 4-6 weeks for delivery of the first issue by mail.

IRNBPAQ309

REQUEST YOUR FREE BOOKS!

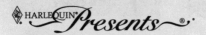

2 FREE NOVELS PLUS
2 FREE GIFTS!

YES! Please send me 2 FREE Harlequin Presents® novels and my 2 FREE gifts (gifts are worth about $10). After receiving them, if I don't wish to receive any more books, I can return the shipping statement marked "cancel." If I don't cancel, I will receive 6 brand-new novels every month and be billed just $4.05 per book in the U.S. or $4.74 per book in Canada. That's a saving of close to 15% off the cover price! It's quite a bargain! Shipping and handling is just 50¢ per book in the U.S. and 75¢ per book in Canada.* I understand that accepting the 2 free books and gifts places me under no obligation to buy anything. I can always return a shipment and cancel at any time. Even if I never buy another book, the two free books and gifts are mine to keep forever.

106 HDN E4FN   306 HDN E4FY

Name	(PLEASE PRINT)	
Address		Apt. #
City	State/Prov.	Zip/Postal Code

Signature (if under 18, a parent or guardian must sign)

Mail to the **Harlequin Reader Service:**
IN U.S.A.: P.O. Box 1867, Buffalo, NY 14240-1867
IN CANADA: P.O. Box 609, Fort Erie, Ontario L2A 5X3

Not valid for current subscribers to Harlequin Presents books.

Are you a current subscriber to Harlequin Presents books and want to receive the larger-print edition? Call 1-800-873-8635 today!

* Terms and prices subject to change without notice. Prices do not include applicable taxes. N.Y. residents add applicable sales tax. Canadian residents will be charged applicable provincial taxes and GST. Offer not valid in Quebec. This offer is limited to one order per household. All orders subject to approval. Credit or debit balances in a customer's account(s) may be offset by any other outstanding balance owed by or to the customer. Please allow 4 to 6 weeks for delivery. Offer available while quantities last.

Your Privacy: Harlequin Books is committed to protecting your privacy. Our Privacy Policy is available online at www.eHarlequin.com or upon request from the Reader Service. From time to time we make our lists of customers available to reputable third parties who may have a product or service of interest to you. If you would prefer we not share your name and address, please check here. ☐

Help us get it right—We strive for accurate, respectful and relevant communications. To clarify or modify your communication preferences, visit us at www.ReaderService.com/consumerchoice.

HP10

Former bad boy Sloan Hawkins is back in
Redemption, Oklahoma, to help keep his aunt's
cherished garden thriving and to reconnect with the
girl he left behind, Annie Markham. But when he
discovers his secret child—and that single mother
Annie never stopped loving him—he's determined
that a wedding will take place in the garden
nurtured by faith and love.

Where healing flows...

Look for

The Wedding Garden
by Linda Goodnight

*Available May 2010
wherever you buy books.*

www.SteepleHill.com

Steeple
Hill®
LI87595

HPCNMBPA0410